DRUID

THE EXILE OF

DEIRDRE AND NAOISE

COLIN DUNNE

Colin Dunne

Published by COLIN DUNNE, 2025

This book is a work of fiction. Whilst based on Irish mythology the names, characters, and events in this book are the products of the author's imagination or are used fictitiously. Any similarities to real people or events are entirely coincidental.

DRUID'S PROMISE

First edition. June 2025.

ISBN: 9798287062163

Copyright © 2025 Colin Dunne.

All rights reserved. Neither this book, nor any parts within it may be sold or reproduced in any form without permission.

CONTENTS

MAP	1
CHAPTER 1 - THE SHORES OF LOCH EITE	2
CHAPTER 2 - DÚN AD	17
CHAPTER 3 - DRUID'S PROMISE	29
CHAPTER 4 - THE ATTACK OF THE FACHAN	41
CHAPTER 5 - THE HUNT BEGINS	54
CHAPTER 6 - BATTLE IN THE DEPTHS	67
CHAPTER 7 - AÍFE'S VISION	83
CHAPTER 8 - CELEBRATIONS IN DÚN AD	96
CHAPTER 9 - ECHOES FROM EMAIN MACHA	113
CHAPTER 10 - THE VOYAGE OF FERGUS	131
CHAPTER 11 - PEACE DISTURBED	145
CHAPTER 12 - THE WEIGHT OF OATHS	163

CHAPTER 13 - CROSSING THE NORTHERN SEA	184
BACKGROUND	196
NAMES	197
CHARACTERS	198
PLACES	202
THE FAMILY OF DEIRDRE AND NAOISE	206
THE WIVES AND CHILDREN OF CONCHOBAR MAC NESSA	207
THE ROYAL FAMILY OF ULAID	208
THE HIGH-KINGS OF ULAID	209
ABOUT THE AUTHOR	210

MAP

North-Western Éirinn and South-Western Alba

Chapter 1

The Shores of Loch Eite

Deirdre sat at the edge of Loch Eite, her eyes fixed on the child that splashed in the shallows. The gentle lapping of waves against the shore mingled with delighted giggles, a melody that both soothed and stirred Deirdre's heart. A cool breeze rustled through the surrounding pines, carrying with it the scent of heather and salt.

As she watched the child play, Deirdre's hand unconsciously drifted to the silver crescent around her neck, a constant reminder of the life she'd left behind. Raised in seclusion with her grandmother in the quaint roundhouse with a red door, she cherished the joyful days spent in her secret garden in the forest, a happy time before she was crushed by the weight of a druid's prophecy. The pendant seemed heavier today, as if the metal itself carried the burden of her thoughts.

She thought of her mother, Aífe, whose name she had given to her daughter. Though time had blurred the lines of her face, Deirdre still remembered the warmth of her voice and the way she would hum as she worked, hands deftly weaving cloth or grinding herbs into fragrant pastes. Her mother had been gentle, but not weak, there was a quiet strength in her, one Deirdre hoped she had inherited.

And then there was her father, Fedlimid, the man whose joy at her birth had quickly turned to sorrow. His deep voice, the scent of heather and pine clinging to his woollen cloak, the way he had once lifted her high onto his shoulders so she could see the world from above. He who wove stories as easily as others wove cloth, but in the end, his words had not been enough to save her from the prophecy that tore her from his arms.

But it was Dáire, her little brother, whom she thought of most painfully. He had been only a toddler when she last saw him, his chubby hands grasping at the hem of her dress as they played. He would be grown now, a man she would not recognize, and who might not remember her at all. Did he ever wonder about the sister he had lost? Or had she faded into nothing more than a whisper of the past, a name spoken only in hushed voices when the fire burned low?

Aífe shrieked with laughter, jolting Deirdre from her thoughts. She forced herself to smile, to push away the ache of what had been and focus on what remained. Her daughter was here, alive and safe, and that had to be enough.

"Aoibhgréine, my love, don't go too deep," Deirdre called out, her voice gentle but firm. The child turned, flashing a smile like the sun that made Deirdre's heart swell.

How quickly she grows, Deirdre mused. And how fiercely I love her. The intensity of her feelings sometimes frightened her, for she knew all too well how love could be wielded as a weapon by those in power.

A movement at the forest's edge caught Deirdre's eye. Naoise emerged from the treeline, his broad shoulders bearing the weight of a freshly killed stag. Even from a distance, she could see the pride in his stance, the satisfaction of a successful hunt evident in every step.

As he drew closer, Deirdre allowed herself a moment to admire him. His raven-black hair was tousled by the wind, and a light sheen of sweat glistened on his brow. His beard, dark and trimmed neatly, was a striking contrast to the golden torc which adorned his neck. The years of their exile had only served to hone his already impressive physique.

"Dad!" Aífe cried out, abandoning her water play to race towards her father.

Naoise's face broke into a wide grin. "Careful now, little one," he cautioned, dropping his spear to one side, his voice rich and warm. "Your old father's a bit weighed down at the moment."

Deirdre couldn't help but smile at the exchange. "A fine catch," she remarked as Naoise approached. "The gods have blessed your hunt today."

Naoise's sea-grey eyes met hers, filled with warmth and a hint of mischief. "Aye, but not half so fine as the catch I made when I won your heart, my love."

A blush crept up Deirdre's cheeks, and she shook her head in mock exasperation. "Save your silver tongue for the king's feasts, Naoise. There's work to be done if we're to eat tonight."

As Naoise hung the deer, Deirdre found her gaze drawn back to the loch. Its placid surface belied the currents that ran deep beneath, much like the undercurrents of her own thoughts.

"What troubles you, love?" Naoise's voice cut through her reverie. "Your eyes are as distant as Tír na nÓg."

Deirdre sighed, unsure how to voice the nameless dread that had been growing in her heart. "It's nothing," she said at last. "Just the fancies of a foolish woman."

Naoise sat down beside her, his presence as comforting as a warm hearth on a cold night. "Your fancies have saved us more than once," he said softly. "Tell me."

Deirdre closed her eyes, letting the sounds of the loch wash over her. "I fear this peace cannot last," she whispered. "The wheel of fate turns ever onward, and I cannot shake the feeling that it may yet crush us beneath it."

Naoise's arm encircled her waist, pulling her close. "Then we shall face it together," he vowed, his voice as steady as the ancient stones that dotted the landscape. "Whatever comes, my heart, we are one."

As Deirdre leaned into his embrace, she tried to let his confidence bolster her own. Yet even as the warmth of his body seeped into hers, she couldn't quite banish the chill that had taken root in her soul. The loch stretched out before them, vast and unknowable, much like the future that awaited them.

The tender moment between Deirdre and Naoise was broken by the sound of raucous laughter approaching from the forest path. Deirdre turned, her golden hair catching the fading sunlight, to see Ardan and Ainnle emerging from the trees.

"Ho there, brother!" Ardan called out, his blue eyes twinkling with mirth. "I see you've managed to fell a beast without our aid. Will wonders never cease?"

Naoise grinned, his arm still wrapped around Deirdre's waist. "Perhaps if you spent less time jesting and more time honing your skills, you'd have brought down your own stag by now."

Ainnle, ever the quieter of the twins, offered a small smile. "We brought something of our own," he said, holding up a woven basket filled with wild berries and mushrooms.

Deirdre felt a warmth bloom in her chest at the sight of the brothers' easy camaraderie. It was moments like these that made their exile bearable, even sweet at times. Yet she couldn't help but wonder how long it would last.

"Come," she said, forcing cheer into her voice. "Let's prepare the evening meal together. Aífe will be hungry after her water play."

As the group moved towards the cluster of three humble roundhouses set back from water's edge, Ainnle sidled up to Deirdre. "You seem troubled, Deirdre," he said, his tone softer now. "Are the old ghosts haunting you again?"

Deirdre met his gaze, seeing the concern beneath his jovial exterior. "Not ghosts," she replied. "More like shadows of what's to come. But let us not dwell on such things now. Tell me of your foraging adventures instead."

As Ardan launched into a tale of their day, embellishing wildly to Ainnle's quiet amusement, Deirdre allowed herself to be caught up in the moment. Yet even as she laughed at Ardan's antics, a part of her remained vigilant, watching the horizon for the storm she feared was gathering.

The family gathered around the fire pit, their movements practiced and harmonious as they set about preparing the evening meal. Deirdre expertly skinned the stag while Naoise and his brothers cleaned and sectioned the meat. Aífe, eager to help, collected herbs from their small garden.

Ardan, his hands busy with the task of sharpening cooking skewers, glanced at Deirdre. "You've become quite the huntress yourself, sister. I remember a time when you couldn't swing a sling."

Deirdre's lips quirked in a wry smile. "Necessity breeds skill, Ardan. Our life here demands it."

As the meat sizzled over the fire, filling the air with a savoury aroma, the family settled around the flames. Naoise passed around wooden plates laden with venison and foraged greens.

"To King Árd-Greimne," Ainnle said, raising a horn of mead. "May his reign continue to offer us sanctuary."

A moment of sombre silence fell over the group before Ardan cleared his throat. "Speaking of our gracious host, I've heard whispers of unrest among the neighbouring clans. It seems our presence here hasn't gone unnoticed."

Naoise's brow furrowed. "What sort of whispers?"

Ardan's usually mirthful eyes were grave as he replied, "There's talk of alliances shifting. Some clans view us as a threat, believing we hold too much sway with Árd-Greimne."

Deirdre felt a chill run down her spine, despite the warmth of the fire. "And what does the king say of this?"

"He maintains his support for us," Ardan said, "but I fear his position may be weakening. The clans grow restless, and there are those who would use our exile as a pretext for conflict."

Naoise's jaw tightened. "We've brought nothing but loyalty and service to Árd-Greimne. Surely that counts for something."

"Aye," Ardan nodded, "but politics is a fickle beast. Our very presence here upsets the balance of power, whether we intend it or not."

As the conversation turned to strategies and potential allies, Deirdre found her gaze drawn to Aífe, peacefully dozing by the fire. The child's innocence stood in stark contrast to the weighty matters being discussed, and Deirdre felt a fierce surge of protectiveness.

"We must be prepared," she said, her voice cutting through the brothers' debate. "For whatever may come. Our family's safety must be our priority."

The men fell silent, the gravity of Deirdre's words settling over them like a shroud. As they continued their meal, the jovial mood of earlier was replaced by a tense undercurrent, each lost in thoughts of what the future might hold.

Deirdre's fingers curled around her wooden cup, her knuckles white with tension. The fire crackled, casting dancing shadows across the faces of her family as they continued their discussion. Her eyes unfocused, mind drifting to the visions that had plagued her sleep for weeks.

A pyre on a hilltop. A raven's harsh cry. The clash of iron on iron.

She shook her head, trying to dispel the images. Naoise's warm hand on her arm startled her back to the present.

"Are you well, my love?" he asked, brow furrowed with concern.

Deirdre managed a wan smile. "Just... lost in thought."

Ainnle leaned forward, his eyes glinting with curiosity. "What troubles you? You've been quiet as a mouse all evening."

She hesitated, weighing her words carefully. "I fear... I fear that our peace here is fragile. That the threads of fate are drawing tighter around us."

"Ah, not this again," Ardan sighed, though his tone was gentle. "Your visions have been wrong before, Deirdre."

"And right too often for comfort," she countered, her voice barely above a whisper.

Naoise squeezed her hand. "Come fire or fate, we face it together. As we have from the first."

As night deepened, the mood gradually lightened. Ainnle produced a small harp, its strings glimmering in the firelight. Soon, the air was filled with music and laughter as they shared stories of their youth in Cnoc Uisneach.

"Do you remember," Ardan chuckled, "when Naoise tried to impress the blacksmith's daughter by lifting her father's anvil?"

Naoise groaned good-naturedly. "How was I to know it was nailed to the floor?"

Deirdre found herself swept up in the warmth of the moment, her earlier fears receding like mist before the sun. As Aífe crawled into her lap, yawning widely, she marvelled at the strength of the bonds between them all.

"Mam, tell me a story," Aífe mumbled sleepily.

Deirdre smiled, stroking her daughter's hair. "Very well, little one. Shall I tell you of Lugh of the Long Arm, and how he won his place among the Tuatha Dé?"

As she wove the tale, Deirdre felt a renewed sense of purpose. Whatever trials lay ahead, they would face them together, as a family. Love and loyalty, these were the weapons they would wield against the encroaching darkness.

The fire dwindled to embers, casting long shadows across the clearing. Deirdre's voice trailed off as she finished her tale, Aífe's soft snores the only response. The night air grew chill, and Deirdre shivered, her gaze drawn inexorably to the dark waters of Loch Eite.

"I'll take her to bed," Naoise murmured, gently lifting their sleeping daughter.

Deirdre nodded, her eyes never leaving the loch. As the others retired, she remained, transfixed by the inky blackness that seemed to pulse with an otherworldly energy.

"The water calls to you," Ainnle observed, settling beside her.

"It whispers secrets," Deirdre replied, her voice distant. "Terrible secrets."

A chill wind swept across the loch, carrying with it the scent of decay. Deirdre's skin prickled, goosebumps rising along her arms.

"What do you see?" Ainnle pressed, concern etching his features.

Deirdre shook her head, struggling to articulate the dread that coiled in her chest. "Nothing yet. But it's coming, Ainnle. I can feel it."

"We've faced worse," he reminded her, his hand warm on her shoulder.

"Have we?" Deirdre whispered, her blue eyes reflecting the dying firelight. "Or will we be swept away like leaves before a storm?"

Ainnle had no answer, and soon he too retired, leaving Deirdre alone with her thoughts. As exhaustion finally claimed her, she retreated to the roundhouse and curled up beside Naoise, her dreams swiftly turning to nightmares.

In her vision, Deirdre stood upon a rocky shore, waves lapping at her feet, a red moon overhead. The water, once clear, began to darken, a crimson stain spreading outward from the horizon. She watched in horror as the blood-red tide surged forward, swallowing islands whole.

"Naoise!" she cried out, but her voice was lost in the roar of the advancing sea.

The tide reached her ankles, warm and viscous. Deirdre tried to run, but her legs refused to move. As the red water rose inexorably, she saw faces in its depths, Conchobar, his eyes burning with possessive rage; Éogan mac Durthacht, his sword dripping with blood; a redheaded giant, weeping tears of betrayal; and worst of all, Naoise and Aife, their lifeless bodies drifting in the bloody current.

"No," Deirdre whimpered, tears streaming down her face as the tide rose to her chest. "Please, Macha, Dagda, anyone... help us."

But no gods answered her plea as the red sea consumed her, dragging her down into its terrible depths.

Deirdre's eyes flew open, a strangled gasp escaping her lips as she bolted upright. Her heart hammered against her ribs, each breath coming in ragged pants. Sweat clung to her brow, golden hair tangled and wild. The embers of the fire cast eerie shadows across the walls of their modest dwelling.

"Naoise?" she whispered, her voice trembling.

Her husband stirred beside her, his strong arm instinctively reaching out to pull her close. "What is it, my love?" he murmured, sleep still heavy in his voice.

Deirdre pressed herself against him, drawing comfort from his solid presence. "A dream," she said, struggling to keep her voice steady. "A terrible dream."

Naoise's eyes opened fully, concern etched across his rugged features. "Tell me," he urged gently.

She shook her head, the horrific images still too vivid.

"A red tide," Deirdre managed, her fingers pressing against Naoise's chest. "Swallowing everything... everyone."

"It was just a nightmare," Naoise soothed, though a flicker of unease passed through his eyes. "We're safe here in Alba."

Deirdre wanted to believe him, but the dread clung to her like a shroud. "But for how long?" she whispered.

As the first pale light of dawn crept through the shutters, Deirdre rose quietly, careful not to wake Naoise or little Aífe. She stepped outside, the cool morning air a balm to her flushed skin. The loch stretched before her, its waters calm and innocent in the growing light.

"I won't let it happen," Deirdre vowed, her voice barely audible. She thought of Aífe's laughter, of Naoise's loving gaze, of the life they had built here. "Whatever comes, I'll protect them."

A gentle breeze stirred her hair, carrying the scent of heather and pine. Deirdre squared her shoulders, lifting her chin in defiance of the fate that had haunted her since birth.

"Let the red tide come," she declared, her blue eyes flashing with determination. "We've faced worse and survived. We are a family, and we will not be broken."

As the morning sun rose fully, painting the world in gold, Deirdre turned back to their home. There was work to be done, a family to care for, a life to live. Whatever storms lay on the horizon, she would face them with the same strength that had carried her this far.

She paused at the threshold, casting one last glance at the peaceful loch. "We make our own destiny," Deirdre whispered, a prayer and a promise.

Chapter 2

Dún Ad

The small currach sailed through the choppy waters of the loch, its leather and wooden frame creaking with each swell. Naoise stood at the prow, his raven hair whipping in the salt-laden wind as he gazed at the rocky outcrop that rose like a jagged beast out of the churning waves. The stone walls of Dún Ad loomed atop the craggy cliffs, a formidable silhouette against the cloudy sky.

As they tied the currach to the wharf, they couldn't help but notice the gulls perched along the harbour wall. The seabirds were all eerily quiet and appeared fearful. Ainnle spoke to the group, "The gulls are behaving strangely. Must be a storm approaching." Ardan simply shrugged his shoulders and said with a smile, "Well, if a storm does come, at least we can shelter at the inn for a few days."

Naoise ignored the chatter of his brothers and focused on Deirdre, his piercing sea-grey eyes softening. "I hope you find some peace," he said, his lyrical voice tinged with concern. "We'll return once we've spoken with the king."

Deirdre nodded, her golden hair gleaming even in the muted light. "Be careful, my love," she whispered, her blue eyes searching his face. "I have an uneasy feeling today."

Naoise smiled, though it didn't quite reach his eyes. "Fear not, my heart. We'll be back before you know it."

After a farewell embrace, they continued past the sailors and merchants of the busy harbour. The cobblestone path winding through the fishing village echoed with Deirdre's soft footsteps, Aífe's small hand clasped tightly in hers. Deirdre's azure eyes darted warily from thatched roof to wooden door, her heart a tumultuous sea of worry.

"Mam, why did the king summon Dad?" Aífe's innocent query pierced through Deirdre's brooding.

"He has an important task for your father and your uncles," Deirdre explained.

"Why Dad though? Surely the king has plenty of warriors to choose from," Aífe probed.

"Remember that we are guests here, and it is our duty to be of use to the king," Deirdre explained.

"Is it because of Dad's geas, that he cannot refuse someone who asks for aid?" Aífe asked with curiosity. She had heard of her father's geas before, a powerful oath that could not be broken without dire consequences.

"No, my dear child, his geas obliges him accept to requests from maids, to refuse such a request would dishonour him and weaken him" Deirdre replied.

"Well that's good to know," Aife said with a smile.

"And who is the old lady we are going to see?" Aife then questioned.

Deirdre managed a weak smile, her golden tresses catching the late afternoon sun. "Ethniu is a druid, little one. She might help me understand some... puzzling dreams."

"Are you sick?" Aife asked with concern.

"No, I'm perfectly fine," Deirdre assured her with a nod.

"Lady Deirdre!" A gruff voice called out from behind, and she turned to see a familiar figure striding towards her.

"Captain Fiach," she greeted, a genuine smile softening her worried features. "What brings you to these shores?"

The weathered sailor approached, his skin tanned and leathery from years at sea. "Ach, can't an old sea dog pay a visit without arousing suspicion?" He winked, then turned his attention to the child at Deirdre's side.

"And who might this wee lass be?" Fiach asked, his voice softening.

Deirdre placed a hand on her daughter's shoulder. "This is Aífe Aoibhgréine, my daughter. Aífe, this is Captain Fiach. He's an old friend who helped your father and me long ago."

Aífe looked up at the towering sailor, her eyes wide with curiosity. "Did you really sail across the whole sea?"

Fiach let out a hearty laugh. "Aye, lass, that I did. And I've got tales that would curl your hair, if it weren't already so bouncy!"

As Aífe giggled, Deirdre felt a warmth spread through her chest. Fiach's presence was like a balm, easing the tension that had coiled within her for days. Yet, as she met the captain's eyes, she saw a flicker of something, concern perhaps? That told her his visit wasn't merely social.

A group of children playing on the shore caught Aífe's attention. "Can I go play, Mam? Please?"

Deirdre hesitated, then nodded. "Stay beside the crannóg, my love. I shan't be too long."

As her daughter scampered off to play by the water's edge, Deirdre turned to Fiach, her voice low. "What news do you bring, old friend? I can see it weighing on you."

Fiach's weathered face creased with concern as he leaned in closer, his voice barely above a whisper. "Trouble brews in Ulaid, Deirdre.

The winds carry whispers of unrest, and King Conchobar's obsession with you burns as fiercely as ever."

Deirdre's breath caught in her throat, her fingers unconsciously tracing the outline of the crescent pendant hidden beneath her tunic, a gift from Leabharcham, her grandmother and mentor. "After all these years?" she murmured, her blue eyes clouding with a mix of disbelief and fear.

"Aye," Fiach nodded grimly. "The old wolf's hunger hasn't waned. He has summoned merchants, travellers, sailors, offering rewards for any whisper of your whereabouts."

A chill ran down Deirdre's spine, and she glanced instinctively towards Aífe, laughing with the other children. The weight of the prophecy that had shaped her life seemed to press down on her shoulders once more.

"What of the people?" she asked, her voice tight with concern. "Surely they don't support this madness?"

Fiach shook his head. "The common folk care little for the politics of kings, all they want is to be left in peace. Some of the nobles whisper of rebellion, but they won't dare face the Red Branch in battle..." He trailed off, leaving the dire implications unspoken.

Deirdre's mind raced, memories of her sheltered life in Ulaid flashing before her eyes. She thought of Naoise, of the life they'd built here, of Aífe who had never known the shadow of Conchobar's obsession.

"We can't run forever," she whispered, more to herself than to Fiach. Her hands clenched at her sides, a fire kindling in her eyes. "Perhaps it's time we faced this threat head-on."

Fiach raised an eyebrow, a mix of admiration and concern in his gaze. "That's dangerous talk, lass. But if anyone has the strength to change fate, it's you and Naoise."

"I truly hope so," Deirdre said as Fiach bowed and took his leave.

* * *

The three brothers pulled their woollen cloaks tight to protect against the relentless coastal wind, as they made their ascent up the winding path to the hilltop fortress

Ardan's voice carried a note of levity as they climbed. "I hope King Árd-Greimne's hospitality includes a warm fire and some mead. I'm chilled to the bone!"

Ainnle, ever the cautious one, spoke softly. "We should be on our guard, brothers. We know not what task the king requires of us."

Naoise nodded, his hand instinctively resting on the hilt of his sword. "Aye, Ainnle speaks true. But we are sons of Uisneach, and we face whatever comes together."

As they approached the gates of the fortress, Naoise gazed down the hill catching a glimpse of Deirdre and Aífe in the village below, their golden hair catching the sunlight. He knew that he must keep the king on their side, for their safety and well-being, a familiar burden settling on his shoulders.

A group of men sat huddled at the top of the hill, appearing distraught and engaged in conversation. Fishermen, Naoise presumed. As the brothers strolled towards the entrance of the grand roundhouse, the men watched them cautiously, filled with curiosity.

The massive doors groaned open, revealing a grand hall filled with the nobles and warriors of Earraghail. The air was thick with the smell of peat smoke and tension. Naoise led his brothers to an empty bench, acutely aware of the many eyes upon them.

At the far end of the hall sat King Árd-Greimne, his weathered face etched with the lines of many battles. To his right, a woman clad in armour resembling fish scales studied the new arrivals with sharp eyes. Her hand rested nonchalantly on the hilt of her sword. To the king's left sat a young maiden, no older than Aífe.

Ardan leaned close to Ainnle, whispering, "Who do you reckon the warrior woman is?"

Ainnle shrugged, his blue eyes twinkling with curiosity. "Whoever she is, I'd wager she's as deadly with that blade as she is fair to look upon."

Naoise shifted uncomfortably in his seat. "Brothers, please. Now is not the time for such talk."

As the last of the assembly took their places, Árd-Greimne, the King of Earraghail rose, his voice booming through the hall. "Sons of Uisneach, you honour us with your presence once more. You came to me over a decade ago seeking refuge. You had travelled far and faced many perils. I granted you protection and a place to call home, even though some counselled against it."

"And for that, you forever have our gratitude, my king," Naoise said.

There were murmurs of discontent in the assembly.

The woman beside the king leaned forward, her voice sharp as steel. "If I were here back then, you would not have been allowed to stay. Why should our people risk the wrath of Conchobar mac Nessa for your sake?"

Naoise's heart raced, but his voice remained steady. "My lady, we committed no crime. We seek only to live in peace, away from those who would tear us apart."

"Enough, this matter has been long settled," the king said firmly. "My friends, excuse the interruption; let me introduce you to my daughter Scáthach and my granddaughter Uathach, they are visiting me from their island fortress in the north," he said turning back to address Clan Uisneach.

The king continued, "Clan Uisneach, I have summoned you for a task suited to your abilities, my people and their livelihoods are under threat. A beast has been attacking the smallfolk up and down the coast, and there was an attack in the loch just this morning, before you arrived," he gestured to warden at the doorway, who immediately pulled open the great doors.

The commotion at the entrance of the roundhouse drew all eyes. Three fishermen stumbled forward, their clothes still damp and clinging to their trembling bodies. The eldest among them, a weathered man with a salt-and pepper beard, fell to his knees before the king.

"Your majesty," he gasped, his voice quavering. "We've come... we've come to beg for your help."

Naoise leaned forward, his brow furrowed. The fear etched on the fishermen's faces sent a chill down his spine.

King Árd-Greimne's expression darkened. "Speak, Finnian. Recount your tale to my guests."

Finnian's eyes darted around the room, as if expecting the threat to materialize at any moment. "It's the loch, m'lord. There's... there's somethin' in it. A monster, the likes o' which we've nae seen in a generation."

"We were oot on our boats," Finnian continued, his words tumbling out in a rush. "The nets were heavy with fish when it came. Like a great grey shadow, twice the length o' a full-grown man, wi' teeth sharp as daggers and a single glowin' eye peerin' up from the depths, like Balor himself had returned. It had hands, aye, but nae arms… and one huge leg that kicked it through the water like a bolt o' lightning. It tore through our nets like spider's thread and pulled two boats under, just like that. It's the Fachan, m'lord, the beast the auld tales warned us aboot!"

The youngest fisherman, barely more than a boy, spoke up. "We lost good men today, Your Majesty. And if we can't fish... our families will starve."

King Árd-Greimne listened intently, his expression grave. Naoise could see the weight of responsibility settling on the monarch's shoulders. He felt a kinship with the king in that moment, remembering the burdens he had borne as a prince of Cnoc Uisneach.

"Thank you, Finnian, you and your brave men eat well and rest, you have earned it," the king said as the fisherfolk walked slowly to the empty bench beside the central hearth.

"This creature, the Fachan" the king said slowly, looking around his hall, "it threatens not just our fisherfolk, but the very survival of our people." He turned, his gaze falling upon Naoise and his brothers. "Sons of Uisneach, you come to me seeking a home. Here is your chance to prove your worth once again. I task you with investigating this threat and ridding our waters of this monster. Proving wrong anyone who doubts my faith in you."

Naoise's heart swelled with a mix of pride and trepidation. He opened his mouth to accept, but was cut off by a sharp voice.

"Father, you cannot be serious!" Scáthach stood, her hand on the hilt of her sword. "You put too much trust in these men and their skills. How can you entrust them with such a vital task?"

Árd-Greimne held up a hand. "Peace, Scáthach. My warriors have told me tales of the prowess of Clan Uisneach. If even half of what is said is true, they are more than capable."

Naoise stepped forward, his voice ringing clear through the hall. "We accept your charge, King Árd Greimne. By my honour and that of my family, we will not rest until your people are safe."

As he spoke, Naoise felt the familiar fire of purpose igniting within him. Yet beneath it all, a small voice whispered of Deirdre and Aífe, in the village below. He pushed the thought aside. This was the price of sanctuary, and he would pay it gladly.

Chapter 3

Druid's Promise

Deirdre approached the rounded silhouette of the crannóg at the edge of the village, her eyes were drawn to the raven perched atop the thick thatch roof. Deirdre's blue eyes met the bird's black gaze and her mind drifted to the nightmares that had plagued her sleep. Visions of slashing teeth and blood-stained waters, of Aífe screaming and Naoise's face contorted in agony. She shuddered at the thought but then steeled herself and stared defiantly at the raven as she crossed the wooden bridge and towards the druid's door. Before she could knock, it swung open, revealing Ethniu's weathered face, eyes twinkling with ancient wisdom.

"Ah, fair Deirdre," Ethniu's voice was as soothing as a summer breeze. "I've been expecting you. Come in, child."

Deirdre stepped into the warmth of the crannóg, the scent of herbs and peat smoke enveloping her. "You... knew I was coming?"

Ethniu chuckled, gesturing for Deirdre to sit by the stone hearth. "The winds whisper many secrets to those who listen. But more importantly, I see the shadows beneath your eyes," she said with a wink and a smile." What troubles your sleep, dear one?"

Deirdre sank onto a wooden stool, her hands twisting in her lap. "I have been dreaming of the past, of Naoise's parents, Uisneach and Ailbhé, of Cú Glas, and the folk of Cnoc Uisneach, all those who perished... so that I might live."

"I have tried talking to Naoise, but he will not speak of it, I fear the pain is too much, "she added with a heavy heart.

"All my life my dreams have haunted me. They say my grandfather Daill the Blind could see the future when he slept," Deirdre confessed. "But lately the dreams are getting worse, nightmares, Ethniu. Terrible visions of... I fear for Aífe and Naoise, for all of us." Deirdre confessed.

The old druid's face grew solemn as she stirred a pot of tea. "Aye, the past casts long shadows to the future. But remember, Deirdre, even the darkest night gives way to dawn."

"What do you mean?" Deirdre leaned forward, her voice barely above a whisper. "Is there truly danger coming?"

Ethniu reached across the space between them, her touch as light as moth wings, yet grounding as the ancient oaks that stood sentinel outside. "Child," she began, her voice rich with the timbre of fallen leaves and wisdom long buried in loamy soil, "all life is but a tapestry of interlaced threads. Each choice, each breath, weaves into the next, creating a pattern vast and wondrous."

"Yet, how does one choose rightly when the weave tightens around the heart?" Deirdre pressed, her eyes searching the druid's for an anchor.

"By understanding that fate is not the enemy," Ethniu replied, her tone imbuing the very air with tranquillity. "It is the dance of possibility, the embrace of the unknown. You must trust in the cycles that govern us, in the ebb and flow that shapes our days."

With a slow exhalation, Deirdre nodded, allowing the druid's words to seep into her marrow, soothing the tremors of uncertainty. Ethniu rose then, her movements deliberate, as if every step she took was etched into the earth's memory.

"Come," Ethniu beckoned, her eyes reflecting the flicker of flames that seemed to burn brighter at her command. "We shall seek guidance from the beyond, listen to the whispers of the Sídhe."

In the hushed sanctum of the crannóg, Ethniu gathered sacred herbs, their scent mingling with the salt-tinged breeze wafting through the woven reed walls. She arranged them meticulously around a shallow stone basin, each placement a silent verse in an unseen hymn.

Deirdre observed, her senses heightened as Ethniu began to chant, the language older than the hills themselves. The syllables twisted and twined like ivy, wrapping around their souls, guiding them toward the veiled threshold of divination.

Ethniu struck flint to iron, sparks cascading into the basin, igniting the herbs. A plume of smoke billowed forth, coiling skyward with serpentine grace. The druid's hands danced above the rising fumes, shaping symbols that shimmered in the air with her fingers, ogham runes that spoke of protection, wisdom, and the unyielding strength of maternal love.

"Breath in deep and see the forms that take shape within the mists," Ethniu murmured, her eyes half-closed in reverence. "Let them reveal what lies beneath the cloak of night, what paths may yet unfurl before your feet."

Deirdre inhaled the vapours and watched, entranced, as visions swirled before her, a tapestry of light and shadow playing upon the canvas of her fears. In the ritual's embrace, she sought the courage to confront whatever may come, guided by Ethniu's unwavering presence and the immutable bonds of family loyalty that fortified her spirit.

The smoke thickened and roiled, a living entity whispering secrets as it ensnared Deirdre in its ethereal grasp. Ethniu's hands continued their silent ballet, coaxing the mists into forms both mesmerizing and terrifying. There, amidst the dance of shadow and light, Emain Macha appeared, strong and unyielding, until flames, fierce and hungry, devoured the hilltop.

"Emain Macha, it burns," Deirdre gasped, her voice a fragile wisp lost in the tumult of the vision. The capital of Ulaid was a pyre, engulfed in a ravenous inferno, its might reduced to cinders before her eyes. It was an omen that clawed at her heart, a harrowing echo of the prophecy that had haunted her since birth.

"Fire consumes," Ethniu intoned, her gaze locked with Deirdre's, "but it also cleanses. In its wake, new life can emerge, yet such rebirth comes not without cost."

Deirdre's breath caught as the smoke shifted, forming shadows that flickered in her sight. Then, like water parting, another vision took shape.

A fair child stood alone upon a blood-darkened shore, slight and slender, golden hair tangled with sweat, sword drawn. A large dark shape appeared in the mists, a warrior proud and mighty.

Deirdre gasped as she saw the battle unfold, swift and terrible. Blades flashed, feet twisted in the sand, and the crash of iron upon iron rang through the vision like a thunder. The young warrior fought with the fury of hound, but wheel of fate had already spun its doom. A bronze spear drove through the child's slender chest and a single, broken cry echoed across the sea.

The mist swirled once more, and the image dissolved. Deirdre reeled, her breath ragged, the taste of prophecy bitter upon her tongue. When the smoke cleared, she whispered a name, a warning that would never reach in time.

"Aífe," Deirdre said with terror in her voice. "I saw Aífe's death on the shores of Ulaid."

As the vision dissolved, leaving only traces in the smoke, a shiver coursed through Deirdre's body. The dread of the prophecy mingled with the protective fire that blazed within her. She would stand against the tides of destiny if need be, for Aífe, for Naoise, for all those bound to her by blood and love.

"The visons you see are but one possible future, but they may be averted," the druid spoke, the weight of ages in her voice. "This prophecy will not come to pass if Aífe never treads upon the soil of Éirinn. You must promise me this."

"I promise Ethniu, I will save Aífe from this fate, she will never sail to Éirinn" Deirdre said, her tone steadier than she felt. "We must remain here in Alba, no matter the cost."

Her resolve crystallized like the ice that clung to the craggy cliffs in winter. She would shield her family from whatever darkness loomed on the horizon, even if it meant defying gods and men.

Ethniu nodded, her wise eyes reflecting the dying light of the ritual's embers. "The path ahead is fraught with shadows and thorns, child. But remember, even in the darkest night, the moon and stars above guide us. Trust in your strength and the bonds that bind your spirit to those you cherish."

Deirdre stood for a moment in the lingering haze, her silhouette etched against the backdrop of Ethniu's sacred space, before taking her leave. The sense of foreboding cast by the visions of Emain Macha ablaze and Aífe's death did little to quench the flame of determination that now burned within her. For her family, for Aífe, she would face whatever perils lay ahead, guided by love and the unyielding force of a mother's will.

As she crossed the bridge of the crannóg, her visons settled on her shoulders like a cloak. The village bustled around her, oblivious to the storm brewing on the horizon. She scanned the area for Aífe, her heart lifting at the sight of her daughter's golden curls playing on the sandy beach.

As Deirdre opened her mouth to call to Aífe, a commotion from the direction of the fortress on the hilltop caught her attention. She turned to see nobles and common folk descending the winding path, their expressions grim.

* * *

In the courtyard of Dún Ad, Naoise stood shoulder to shoulder with Ardan and Ainnle, their heads bent close as they discussed the task set before them. The weight of King Árd-Greimne's trust settled upon them like a mantle.

"A sea creature, terrorizing the fishermen," Ainnle mused, his hand resting on the hilt of his sword. "It could be anything from a particularly aggressive seal to... well, something far worse."

Naoise nodded, his sea-grey eyes scanning the horizon. "Whatever it is, we must approach this with caution. The lives of the fisherfolk depend on us."

Ardan, grinned despite the gravity of the situation. "At least it's not another of Conchobar's schemes, eh? I'd rather face a hundred sea monsters than that old tyrant's wrath."

The jest brought a smile to Naoise's face, but it didn't quite reach his eyes. "Let's hope it stays that way, brother. For now, we focus on the task at hand."

Gathering their weapons and supplies, Naoise felt a swell of pride and affection for his brothers. Their loyalty had never wavered, not through their flight from Ulaid, nor through the challenges of building a new life here.

As they turned to leave the fortress, Naoise's thoughts drifted to Deirdre and Aífe, waiting in the village below. He silently vowed to protect the life they had built from any threat, be it monster or man.

The three brothers descended the winding path from Dún Ad, their silhouettes stark against the blazing orange sky. Naoise's eyes lingered on the sea below, its surface a mirror of molten gold in the fading light. The beauty of the moment was tinged with foreboding, and he couldn't shake the feeling that this mission would change everything.

"It's quiet," Ardan murmured, breaking the silence. "Too quiet for my liking."

Naoise nodded, his hand instinctively tightening on the hilt of his sword. "The fishermen's fear has spread."

As they neared the bottom of the crag, the path widened, revealing the expanse of the coastline beyond the village. The waves lapped gently at the shore, but beneath the peaceful facade, Naoise sensed a lurking danger.

"We should check the caves first," Ainnle suggested, gesturing towards the rocky outcroppings. "If this creature's made a lair, that's where we'll find it."

Naoise agreed, but his thoughts were elsewhere. "I must tell Deirdre our mission and I promised Aífe I'd be back after we spoke to the king."

Ardan chuckled. "The fierce warrior, wrapped around his daughter's little finger."

"You'll understand when you have children of your own," Naoise retorted, a smile tugging at his lips despite his concern.

As if summoned by his thoughts, Naoise spotted a group of small figures playing by the loch's edge. Aífe's golden hair shimmered in the dying light, reminding him so much of Deirdre it made his heart ache.

"Speaking of your little princess," Ainnle said, following Naoise's gaze.

Naoise frowned. "Children shouldn't be playing near the water. Not with this threat lurking about."

He quickened his pace, his brothers matching his stride. As they drew closer, Naoise saw Aífe crouched at the loch's edge, her small hand reaching out towards the loch's surface.

"Aífe!" he called out, his voice carrying on the wind. "Step back from the water, my love!"

But Aífe seemed transfixed, her eyes wide with wonder. "Dad, look!" she cried, her voice filled with childish excitement. "I think I see a selkie!"

Aífe's small feet carried her closer to the loch's edge, her excitement palpable in the cool evening air. The surface of the water was unnaturally still, like polished glass reflecting the fading light of day. Not a ripple disturbed its mirror-like facade, save for the gentle lapping at the shoreline.

"Come out, little selkie!" Aífe called, her voice ringing out across the eerie silence. "I want to play with you!"

As she inched closer, the hairs on the back of her neck stood on end. The loch seemed to hold its breath, an unseen tension building beneath its placid surface. Aífe's heart raced with a mixture of excitement and an instinctive, primal fear she couldn't quite understand.

Naoise's voice carried on the wind, urgent and tinged with worry. "Aífe! Get back from the water now!"

But Aífe couldn't tear her eyes away from the dark shape moving beneath the surface. It was larger than any beast she'd ever seen, its form shifting and undulating in ways that defied her young mind's comprehension.

"But Dad," she called back, her voice wavering slightly, "I've never seen a selkie before. It looks so…"

Her words caught in her throat as the shape surged towards her, the water around it beginning to churn and froth. In that moment, Aífe realized with crushing clarity that this was no playful water spirit.

The wonder in her eyes gave way to terror as a monstrous form began to breach the surface, water cascading off smooth skin that gleamed like wet obsidian in the dying light.

Aífe's scream pierced the air, a sound of pure, unadulterated fear that echoed across the loch and sent birds scattering from nearby trees.

"DAD!" she cried out, her little legs frozen in place as the creature rose before her, blocking out what remained of the day's light.

Naoise's heart stopped as he saw the beast towering over his daughter. He broke into a desperate sprint, drawing his scian with a metallic ring that cut through Aífe's terrified cries.

"Hold on, my love!" he shouted, willing his legs to carry him faster. "I'm coming!"

But as Naoise raced towards his daughter, a sinking feeling in his gut told him he might already be too late.

Chapter 4

The Attack of the Fachan

Deirdre stood at the edge of the fishing village, her golden hair whipping in the salty breeze as she gazed out at the loch. The grey waters stretched before her, a mirror of the overcast sky, when a piercing scream shattered the tranquillity. Her heart seized in her chest, recognizing the voice immediately. "Aífe!" she gasped, her face a mask of terror.

Without a moment's hesitation, Deirdre sprinted towards her daughter, her long legs eating up the distance. Her heart thundered in her chest, each beat a prayer to the gods. Please, not my daughter. Not my Aífe.

As she reached the shoreline, her breath caught in her throat. There, in the loch, a monstrous form was rising from the depths. Its single eye gleamed with malevolence, fixed upon a small figure at the water's edge.

"No!" Deirdre cried out, her voice raw with desperation. She could see Aife now, her golden hair so like her own, splashing frantically as the beast approached.

She heard a man's voice ring out from the shore behind her, "By the Dagda's cauldron! It's the Fachan!"

Deirdre barely heard him, her world narrowing to her daughter and the creature threatening her. She ran towards the frigid water, her maternal instinct overriding all sense of self-preservation.

I should have known, she thought bitterly. The prophecy said I would bring ruin. Is this the price of my choices? My daughter's life?

But as ran, ready to fight the beast with her bare hands if necessary, Deirdre felt a fierce determination replace her fear. She had defied kings and prophecies for love. She would defy death itself for her child.

"Hold on, Aífe!" she shouted, her voice carrying across the water. "I'm coming!"

The beast surged forward, its muscular neck arching out of the water. In a heartbeat, massive jaws clamped around Aífe's leg. The child's scream of pain pierced the air, cutting through Deirdre like a blade. The monster began to drag Aífe under, its powerful body churning the water into a frothing chaos. Deirdre could see her daughter's terrified face, her blue eyes wide with fear.

"Aífe!" Deirdre cried, her voice cracking with anguish. She plunged into the loch without hesitation, the icy water shocking her system. But she pushed through, her arms cutting through the waves with desperate strength.

"Hold on, my love!" Deirdre called out, her heart pounding in her ears. She swam harder, each stroke bringing her closer to her child. I won't lose you. Not now, not ever.

As she neared, the Fachan's baleful eye swivelled towards her. For a moment, Deirdre felt paralyzed by its gaze, an otherworldly malevolence radiating from its depths. But Aífe's whimper broke the spell.

"Mam, help me!" Aífe cried, her voice weak and trembling.

Deirdre lunged forward, her fingers grazing Aífe's outstretched hand. "I'm here, my darling. I won't let go."

The monster pulled harder, dragging both of them further from shore. Deirdre could feel the inexorable strength of the beast, its power far beyond her own. But she held on, her grip on Aífe's hand white-knuckled and unyielding.

As the cold water lapped at her chin, Deirdre looked into Aífe's eyes, seeing her own determination reflected there. Danu, lend me your mother's strength, Deirdre prayed silently. Manannán, lord of the seas, calm these waters. Please, any god who listens, save my daughter.

"As they struggled against the beast's might, a familiar voice rang out from the shore. "Aífe!" Naoise's anguished cry carried across the water, filled with fear and desperate love.

Relief flooded Deirdre's veins, but the battle was far from over. The Fachan thrashed violently, its massive form creating waves that threatened to submerge them all. She turned her head, catching sight of her beloved sprinting along the coastline, his brothers Ardan and Ainnle close behind. Their faces were masks of determination, eyes locked on the unfolding drama in the loch.

Deirdre's arms burned with exhaustion, her grip on Aífe weakening. She could feel the monster's relentless pull, dragging them both deeper. "Naoise!" she called back, her voice hoarse. "The monster, it won't let go!"

Naoise's response was lost in the roar of the waves, but Deirdre could see him gesturing frantically to his brothers. The three men moved in perfect synchronization, years of fighting side by side evident in their fluid motions.

As Ardan and Ainnle let lose volley after volley from their slings, Naoise dove into the water without hesitation. His powerful form cut through the waves, closing the distance with inhuman speed.

"Hold on," he shouted, his sea-grey eyes blazing with fierce protectiveness. "I'm coming."

Deirdre felt a surge of hope, watching her husband and his brothers working as one to save their family. The bond between them was palpable, a force as strong as the monster that sought to drag them under.

"We're holding," Deirdre grunted, her grip on Aífe unwavering, as stones rained down on the monster. "But this monster's grip is like iron."

As Naoise drew closer, Deirdre locked eyes with him, drawing strength from his unwavering gaze. Together, she thought, we can overcome anything.

As Ardan and Ainnle let loose their slings, a figure emerged like a shadow from the mist-shrouded shore, her presence as commanding as the storm-tossed waves. Scáthach, the warrior maid of Earraghail, raced past the twins and Ainnle with almost inhuman speed, her chestnut hair streaming behind her like a battle pennant.

The twins were in awe at the warrioress. "Scáthach!" Ardan called out, his voice carrying over the tumult. "The beast has Aífe!"

Scáthach's green eyes flashed with determination as she sprinted along the rocky coastline. Her horn scale armour glinted in the dim light, each movement a testament to years of honed combat skills.

"I see the beast," Scáthach's voice rang out, clear and confident. "Hold the girl tight!"

Without breaking stride, she hurled a javelin with unerring accuracy, its wicked point gleaming with deadly promise. The weapon was a blur of lethal intent, its leather throwing thong screamed like a Bean Sídhe as it flew through the air, embedding itself deep in the monster's thick hide.

The beast roared in pain and fury, its grip on Aífe released. Naoise seized the moment, plunging his scian deep into the Fachan's neck and lunging forward to take his daughter's hand. "We've got you, my love," he murmured, his voice thick with emotion, as together Deirdre and Naoise held Aífe close and began kicking back towards the shore.

As Scáthach waded into the shallows, her sword drawn and gleaming, the monster retreated, leaving a trail of inky blood in its wake. It lingered for a moment, its evil eye fixed on its escaped prey, before sinking into the murky depths.

As they made their way to shore, Naoise couldn't shake the feeling that this was far from over. The Fachan's retreat felt more like a tactical withdrawal than a defeat. We've won this battle, he thought, but the war has only just begun.

Deirdre's heart thundered in her chest as they scrambled back to the water's edge. "Aífe!" she cried, her voice raw with emotion as she sank to her knees, cradling Aífe's limp form against her chest. She brushed wet strands of golden hair from her daughter's face, her touch trembling yet tender. "My brave girl," she whispered, her voice catching. "Open your eyes for me, my love."

Aífe's face was ashen, her lips tinged with blue. "Please wake up," Deirdre begged.

Naoise gazed at his daughter in desperation, "Gods, please help us?" he pleaded.

As if summoned by his words, Ethniu emerged from the gathering crowd. She moved with surprising swiftness for one of her years. Her weathered face was a mask of calm determination as she knelt beside Deirdre and Aífe.

"Let me see her, child," Ethniu said, her voice carrying the weight of ancient wisdom.

Deirdre hesitated, her protective instincts warring with her trust in the druid. "Can you help her?"

Ethniu's eyes, deep pools of understanding, met Deirdre's. "The spirits of earth and water heed my call. I will do all in my power to aid your daughter."

With a nod, Deirdre loosened her grip, allowing Ethniu to place her gnarled hands on Aífe's chest. The druid closed her eyes, her lips moving in a silent incantation. The air around them seemed to thicken, charged with an unseen energy.

Deirdre watched as Ethniu's hands moved with practiced precision, her long fingers pressing down on Aífe's chest in a steady rhythm, the tendons in her fingers taut with effort, her eyes closed in concentration. Deirdre, Naoise and their companions watching in anticipation, their faces etched with concern.

Suddenly, Aífe's body convulsed. Water gushed from her mouth as she coughed and sputtered, each breath more vigorous than the last. Deirdre's heart soared, tears of joy and relief streaming down her face.

"There now," Ethniu murmured, her voice gentle. "Breathe deep, little one. Let the air of life fill your lungs once more."

Aífe's eyelids fluttered, a weak cough wracking her small frame. Relief flooded through Deirdre, mingling with the fear still coiled tightly in her gut.

"Mam?" Aífe's voice was barely a whisper.

"I'm here, darling. You're safe now." Deirdre's words were soft, but laced with iron.

As Aífe's closed her eyes once more and her breathing steadied, Deirdre gathered her close once more, pressing a kiss to her forehead. "Thank you," she whispered to Ethniu, her gratitude beyond measure.

The druid smiled, the lines around her eyes deepening. "It is but my duty and my honour. The child is strong, like her mother." She placed a comforting hand on Deirdre's shoulder and turned her attention to Aífe's other injuries. "She has deep wounds on her thigh and has lost a lot of blood. Carry her to my home, she will need care and rest to fully recover."

Deirdre nodded, her mind already racing with plans to protect Aífe, to keep her safe from further harm. The shadow of the Fachan loomed large in her thoughts, a threat she knew they had not seen the last of.

Deirdre rose, cradling Aífe's limp form against her chest. The child's weight, once a comfort, now felt like an anchor of worry. With each laboured step towards the crannóg, Deirdre's heart thrummed a desperate prayer to Macha, goddess of fertility and protector of children.

The wooden walkway creaked beneath her feet as she approached the circular dwelling rising from the loch's placid surface. Its thatched roof and wattle walls promised sanctuary, a bulwark against the terrors that lurked beneath the water. The raven was nowhere to be seen.

Inside, the air hung heavy with the scent of peat smoke and sweet herbs. Deirdre gently lowered Aífe onto a thick woollen rug beside the stone hearth, its flames casting flickering shadows across her daughter's pale face. Naoise ducked under the low doorway as he followed behind them.

"Will she... will she be alright?" Deirdre's voice cracked, her eyes never leaving Aífe's still form.

Ethniu knelt beside them, her weathered hands hovering over Aífe's body. "The child's spirit is strong, but the Fachan's touch lingers. We must act swiftly."

The druid grabbed her satchel hanging from a post and retrieved a bone needle and spool of catgut thread. She worked with speed and precision, skilfully stitching closed the gashes on Aífe's leg. She then withdrew bundles of herbs and small clay pots. As she began to crush leaves between her fingers, their pungent aroma filled the air.

Deirdre watched, her throat tight with unspoken fears. "What can I do?"

Ethniu's eyes softened. "Hold her hand, speak to her. Your love is a tether to this world."

Nodding, Deirdre clasped Aífe's small hand in her own. "We're here, my darling," she whispered, her voice thick with unshed tears. "We're all waiting for you to open your eyes."

As Ethniu began to chant, her voice low and melodious, Deirdre's mind raced. How could she have let this happen? She had sworn to protect Aífe, to shield her from the dangers that haunt this world. Now, watching her daughter fight for each breath, Deirdre felt the weight of her failure crushing down upon her.

"You mustn't blame yourself," Ethniu said softly, as if reading Deirdre's thoughts. "The ways of the Fachan are beyond mortal understanding."

Deirdre's jaw clenched. "Understanding or not, I'll see that beast destroyed for what it's done."

The druid's hands stilled for a moment. "Vengeance is a perilous path, child. It can consume the heart as surely as any monster."

"And what would you have me do?" Deirdre challenged, her voice low and fierce. "Stand idle while it threatens my family?"

Ethniu resumed her ministrations, her touch gentle on Aífe's brow. "I would have you focus on healing. On love. Those are the forces that will truly protect your child."

As if in response to her words, Aífe stirred, a soft moan escaping her lips. Deirdre leaned forward, hope and fear warring in her chest. "Aoibhgréine? Can you hear me, my love?"

The girl's eyelids fluttered, and Deirdre felt as though her own heart had stopped, waiting for a sign that her daughter would truly return to them.

The tense silence was shattered by the sound of approaching footsteps. Deirdre's gaze snapped to the entrance of the crannóg, where Scáthach now stood, her imposing figure silhouetted against the fading daylight. The warrior maid's green eyes swept over the scene, lingering on Aífe's prone form before settling on Deirdre.

"How fares the child?" Scáthach asked, her voice low and tinged with concern.

Deirdre swallowed hard, fighting to keep her voice steady. "She lives, but... we wait to see if she'll wake."

Scáthach nodded grimly, then stepped fully into the dwelling. Her armour shimmered in the firelight as she moved, each step purposeful and measured. "I've seen this before," she declared, her tone carrying the weight of hard-won experience. "The Fachan, the beast that attacked your daughter it is an Each-Uisce."

Naoise, who had been standing silently by Aífe's side, turned to face her. "Each-Uisce. You know of this creature?"

"Aye," Scáthach replied, her eyes hardening. "The Each-Uisce is a water horse of terrible power and cunning. It lures its victims with their beautiful forms, only to reveal its true nature when it's too late. Those who survive it's bite become it's thralls. The venom festers in the blood, spreading a slow death through the body."

Deirdre felt a chill run down her spine, remembering the monstrous shape that had erupted from the loch. Her fingers tightened around Aífe's small hand. "How do we stop the Fachan's venom, how can we save Aífe?"

Scáthach's lips curved into a fierce smile. "There is but one cure," she said, her voice thrumming with anticipation. "We must hunt the beast and slay it. Only then will its poison lose its grip on Aífe's soul."

Naoise stepped forward, his sea-grey eyes meeting Scáthach's. "You'll join us in this hunt?"

"I will," she nodded, her chestnut hair catching the firelight as she moved. "My javelin tasted its blood today. I mean to finish what I started."

Deirdre felt a surge of gratitude, tinged with a fierce protectiveness. "Thank you," she said softly, she wanted to join the fight against the monster but she rebelled against the idea of leaving Aífe's side.

Scáthach's expression softened slightly as she looked at Deirdre. "Your daughter is strong, like her mother. She'll need that strength in the days to come." Her gaze hardened once more as she turned back to Naoise. "We should leave at first light. The Fachan is wounded and will have retreated to its lair to lick its wounds, but it won't abandon its hunting grounds easily."

As Naoise and Scáthach began to discuss preparations, Deirdre found herself torn. The desire for vengeance burned hot in her chest, urging her to join the hunt. But when she looked down at Aífe's pale face, willing her to open her eyes, Deirdre knew she could not leave her side.

Chapter 5

The Hunt Begins

Naoise stood in the doorway of the crannóg, the gentle breeze ruffling his dark hair and carrying with it the smell of the sea. In front of him, Deirdre sat by Aífe's side, their auras intertwined in a bittersweet embrace. Naoise knew it was time for him to leave, to embark on his journey, but he couldn't bring himself to say the words.

Instead, he knelt down and rubbed his daughter's cheek and whispered in her ear "Rest well my princess, I'll will be back soon".

He turned and gave Deirdre a tight hug. He could feel her body trembling against his, her tears dampening his skin. He didn't want to let go, to leave the safety and comfort of the crannóg and the two women he loved.

"Please Naoise, can you wait until Aífe is fully recovered?" Deirdre pleaded.

"I cannot. I have made a promise to the king to slay this monster. There may be more fisherfolk attacked, more children..." Naoise replied sadly.

So with a heavy heart, he kissed them both on the forehead, whispering words of love and farewell. And then he turned and walked away, his footsteps echoing on the wooden planks of the bridge, his heart heavy with longing and regret.

Naoise's sea-grey eyes met Scáthach's green gaze, the warrior maid standing on the sandy shoreline, her face set with the grim determination of those who have known battle. The wind tugged at Naoise's raven black hair, and he tucked a stray lock behind his ear before speaking.

"Scáthach, your knowledge of these treacherous waters is as a guiding star to us," Naoise said, his voice rich with the lyrical quality that often graced his tongue. "And your prowess in combat is the stuff of legend. With you at our side, I trust we shall hunt down the Fachan and rid these lands of its malevolence."

The warrior maid, her chestnut hair flowing in the sea breeze behind her, nodded solemnly. Naoise observed that her armour was constructed from numerous discs of polished horn, resembling the scales of a fish, which caught the dimming light, casting a lustrous sheen over her formidable frame. "Aye, Naoise mac Uisneach, we shall track the beast to the very edge of Manannán's domain if need be. Our resolve is as the ancient oaks, unyielding."

As the first rays of Lugh's chariot rose above the horizon, the group stood at the harbour, their currachs bobbing in the water like ducks.

Naoise spoke up, "Scáthach and I will venture north to seek out the beast. My brothers, stay vigilant as this is a formidable foe."

Ardan, his brown hair a wild mane around a face marked by freckles and determination, clasped hands with Ainnle, whose own eyes mirrored his twin's courage though his voice seldom carried the same conviction.

"Southward we sail, my brother, do not fear for us. Together, we are a match for any foe," Ardan declared, his tone imbued with warmth and a touch of humour that belied the urgency of their endeavour. Ainnle merely nodded, his silent agreement as steadfast as his presence.

The three brothers shared one final embrace before parting ways.

Naoise and Scáthach turned to prepare the vessel for departure, their movements brisk and efficient. They worked in harmony, gathering supplies and weapons with practiced ease. Amongst the array of armaments, Scáthach handled one particular item with reverence, a long, thin bundle wrapped in oiled leather.

"Your weapon?" Naoise inquired, noting the careful manner in which she treated the mysterious package.

"Indeed," Scáthach replied, allowing a rare smile to grace her lips. "The Gáe Bulg has a thirst for the blood of monsters of the sea, river and loch. It will not be denied."

With no further words needed, Naoise pushed their currach away from the harbour wall and dropped the oars into the surging embrace of the sea, the waves lapping hungrily at the hull. As dawn broke, with the horizon painted in hues of amber and gold, the currachs drifted apart, each bearing a fragment of hope as daylight slowly embraced the land.

* * *

The northern waters stretched before Naoise and Scáthach, their currach slicing through the waves like a keen blade through battle-torn flesh. The coastline loomed like an ancient behemoth, its cliffs jagged teeth against the sky's soft palate. Naoise felt the raw power of this untamed land echo in his chest, a wild rhythm that matched the pulsing of his warrior's heart.

"Beautiful, isn't it?" he said, his voice barely rising above the roar of the sea as they skirted the shoreline.

"Aye, but treacherous as a serpent's whisper," Scáthach replied, her eyes scanning the horizon with the vigilance of a hawk. Her green gaze caught the play of light on water, where sunbeams danced upon the crests of waves like flames upon a pyre.

The salt-laden winds clawed at their cloaks, and Naoise savoured the bracing chill that cut to his bones. It was a clean cold, one that stripped away all pretences, leaving only the essence of life in its wake. His grey eyes, mirrors of the tumultuous sea, watched the shore give way to scattered isles, each a sentinel standing guard over age-old secrets.

As the day waned, the two warriors found respite from the relentless buffeting of the wind behind a cove's natural bulwark. Naoise secured the oars and then stretched his weary back muscles, while Scáthach tethered their vessel to a weather-worn rock, her movements precise and practiced.

"Tell me, Scáthach," Naoise began, his lyrical voice rising above the susurrus of the sea, "how well do you know these lands and waters?"

She leaned against the currach's mast, arms crossed, the contours of her horn armour catching the last rays of the sinking sun. "I was born here, and although I haven't lived in my father's kingdom in quite some time, I still remember every cove and cave. After my mother's passing, this kingdom no longer held any joy for me and I longed to explore the world. Now, I call Sgitheanach home, an isle twenty leagues north, with my daughter Uathach," she explained, gesturing towards the northern waters. "In my fortress of Dún Scáith, I train those who seek mastery in combat."

"Your reputation as a warrior and a teacher precedes you. As of yesterday, I was not aware that King Árd-Greimne had any children, least not you," Naoise acknowledged, nodding with genuine respect.

Scáthach spoke with a hint of sadness in her voice. "My father is a proud man, and he does not approve of my school. He would rather I return to live in Dún Ad with my daughter."

Naoise remarked, "They say that no one leaves your tutelage without iron in their spine and fire in their soul."

"True enough," she said, a flicker of pride warming her stoic expression. "But few are willing to endure what is necessary to wield such strength. It is not the body we must forge anew, but the spirit within."

"Strength of spirit is the mark of true nobility," Naoise mused. "In song and story, the greatest heroes are those whose hearts burn brightest in the face of darkness."

Scáthach regarded him thoughtfully, the sea's reflection dancing in her gaze. "And what of your own tales, Naoise mac Uisneach? What battles have carved your path?"

He smiled, a ghost of mirth playing upon his lips. "There have been many, but none so fierce as the battle for the heart I now fight to protect. Love is a strange and mighty adversary."

Her laughter, rare and unguarded, joined with his in a moment of shared understanding. They were warriors, yes, bound by honour and the relentless pursuit of their quest. But beneath the tempered surface of their resilience, the same human longings whispered, love and loyalty to family.

Naoise then watched as Scáthach's deft hands unwound the leather straps binding the ornate leather bag. With each layer she peeled away, the anticipation thickened like a sea fog rolling onto the shore. Finally, she revealed the instrument of legend cradled within, the Gáe Bulg.

"Behold," she began, her voice as steady as the tides, "the legacy of battles waged not by men but by leviathans of the deep." Naoise's eyes were drawn to the weapon, its bronze head gleaming with an otherworldly patina and bone white spiralling shaft. A leather thong was attached near the foot, its intricate knots whispering of ancient craft.

"This is no mere spear, but a relic of the duel between the Coinchenn and the Curruid."

Scáthach continued with her tale. "After my mother passed away, I convinced a wine merchant to let me join his crew on his galley. I sailed to many lands, from the scorching south to the mystical kingdoms of the east. It was in the great kingdom of Eadaíl, where I met Uathach's father. He was a skilled warrior who taught me valuable lessons.

Together, we ventured to Lochlann, a kingdom located in the far north where ice dominated the sea. It was there that we witnessed the clash of between two colossal sea monsters - the Coinchenn and the Curruid. For two days, they fought fiercely until the Curruid grew tired and was ultimately impaled by the Coinchenn's formidable horn. The following morn the Curruid's broken body washed upon the shore," Scáthach recounted, her green eyes distant as if reliving the moment.

Raising her spear triumphantly, she declared, "From the Curruid's death came this instrument of war. The shaft is made from the tip his mighty horn, it is light, but strong as iron."

"And my armour too," she added striking the gleaming scales on her chest, "was crafted from the horn and skin of the sea monster. No blade can pierce it."

Naoise reached out, his fingers running along the spiralling groves in the shaft wrought from the vanquished beast.

Scáthach then stood up to reveal the final secret of the Gáe Bulg. She looped the leather strap around her thumb, then gripped the shaft near the point. With a flick of her wrist, she released the spear and it flew from her hand like a bolt of lightning. It pierced the thick wooden crossbeam where she was just sitting, causing it to shatter into a shower of splinters. As the dust cleared, seven sharp barbs were now visible on the spearhead, each one capable of piercing a dragon's hide. Scáthach gave the spearhead a twist, and the barbs retracted once more.

"What sorcery is this?" Naoise exclaimed in awe.

"The magic of the gods," she intoned "Goibniu himself cast these deadly barbs when the world was young. "Trust in this, Naoise mac Uisneach, for it shall serve us well against the Fachan."

In that moment, the bond between them was forged stronger than any metal; a trust born of shared secrets and the unveiling of sacred might.

The day waned as they drew near a remote island, shrouded in the silence of impending dusk. Dark clouds brooded overhead, casting a pall over the sea as their currach sliced through the grey waters. A sickly green slime clung to the surface near the shore, algae thick and glistening, swirling lazily in the tidal wash. Jagged rocks rose like the spines of some slumbering behemoth, guarding the approach to cavernous maws gaping along the coastline.

"Those caves," Scáthach murmured, her gaze fixed on the yawning darkness ahead, "they are the threshold between our world and the watery abyss."

Naoise felt a shiver chase down his spine, carried by the chill wind that howled a mournful dirge through the crags. The entrance loomed before them, an abyssal gateway etched into the bones of the earth. Every surge of the relentless tide seemed to beckon them closer, whispering of secrets and dangers entombed within the rock.

"Let us be swift," he said, echoing Scáthach's resolve, his hand resting on the pommel of his sword, a silent vow to protect and prevail.

Druid's Promise

They were kin in purpose, bound by a quest for justice and safeguarded by the threads of loyalty that intertwined their fates. Together, they would brave the shadows and emerge victorious, or fall to legend amidst the echoes of the sea.

Naoise's breath formed clouds in the chill air as he and Scáthach entered the sea caves, their steps echoing against the ancient stone as they dragged the currach out of the waves reach. The cave floor was slick with same slime that choked the shoreline, making each step a cautious negotiation with the treacherous footing.

Quickly he struck flint to his scian, and the spark caught in an instant, licking hungrily at the dry torch-heads. Flames leapt to life, pushing back the gloom that clung to the cave like a living thing. Shadows danced across the hull of the currach as he moved swiftly, unfastening his arms and armour from their bindings.

He wore a tunic of stiffened, boiled leather, its surface darkened from years of use. Around his waist, he tightened his belt with practiced ease, shifting the weight of his sword and scian until they rested just right against his hips.

In his left hand, he bore his round shield, made of alder and calf skin, its surface adorned with the proud sigil of Clan Uisneach, a golden eagle, wings spread wide against a deep blue field. The paint had faded in places, worn by salt air and battle, but the symbol remained defiant. Whenever his eyes fell upon it, he thought of Smóil, his father's eagle, soaring high in the blue skies above Cnoc Uisneach. The thought stirred a deep ache in his chest, a yearning for home that never quite left him.

Shaking his head to regain his focus he picked up his two javelins, gripping them in his shield hand, their slender shafts balanced and ready, their iron tips eager to taste blood.

Standing across from him Scáthach dipped her fingers into a pouch of crushed woad, the deep blue pigment cold against her skin. With slow, deliberate strokes, she painted the swirling lines of her battle paint, symbols of strength, protection, and the death she would bring to those who dared cross her. The woad dried quickly, tightening against her flesh, a second skin of war.

Then she cinched her belt tighter, adjusting her scale armour, the horn plates pressed firm around her body. With fluid grace she drew the Gáe Bulg from its protective leather bag, its bronze head gleamed bright in the torchlight, its ogham runes seeming to thirst for the blood it had yet to spill. She ran her fingers along the shaft, feeling the weight of fate in her grasp. With a flick of her wrist she spun it effortlessly above her head, and swung it down as if striking an invisible foe. Her long chestnut braid swung behind her as she moved, a warrior's rhythm in every motion.

The rugged cave was a labyrinth of shadows and whispers, the walls slick with centuries of weeping moisture. Here, beneath the earth, the world above seemed but a distant memory, its

Druid's Promise

colours leached away by the gloom of the subterranean void.

The torchlight sputtered, casting an orange glow that danced over the walls, revealing carvings so old and worn that time itself appeared to have forgotten their purpose. Towering figures, hewn into the rock with meticulous reverence, depicted monstrous creatures of such grotesque visage that Naoise felt a knot of unease coil within his gut.

"Formorian," Scáthach breathed, her voice barely above a whisper. "These are tales from the dark days, before men came to these shores."

The carvings writhed with depictions of beings with limbs too numerous to count, eyes that bore malice, and mouths filled with dagger-like teeth. They were a pantheon of nightmares, frozen in stone eternities before Scáthach's ancestors had even walked these lands.

"Look here," Scáthach said, her fingers tracing the outline of a figure shrouded in what might have been mist or water, its form was elusive, yet palpably sinister. "This...this beast was not born of nature. This speaks of dark rituals, of blood spilled into the sea to waken hunger in the ancient depths."

Naoise followed her gaze, feeling the weight of her revelation settle upon him. The Fachan, the Each-Uisce, could it be a spawn of such malevolence? A creature summoned not by chance but by design?

"Then our quest bears a gravity beyond the hunt alone," Naoise murmured, his thoughts adrift amidst the waves of implications. "We face not only a beast but the spectre of ancient sorcery."

"Indeed." Scáthach's eyes reflected the flames, a warrior's resolve burning within. "Our blades may strike true, but it is knowledge that will arm us against the tides of this dark past."

A silence settled between them, as heavy as the stones that encased their path. In their hearts, a bond strengthened, woven from the threads of shared purpose and newfound understanding. They stood side by side, warriors of light venturing into the abyss, where the echoes of forgotten gods whispered of battles yet to come.

Chapter 6

Battle in the Depths

Naoise's breath materialized in the frigid air as he and Scáthach stepped into the belly of the sea caves, the rhythmic crash of distant waves a ghostly chorus to their intrusion. Their footfalls, muffled by the damp seaweed beneath them, echoed against the jagged stone walls, rebounding off the cavern's gullet like whispers of warning.

"Keep close," Naoise advised, his grey eyes as dark as the shadows that danced at the edge of their torchlight. The air was a thick, stagnant cloak, heavy with salt and the cloying, iron taint of decay. Each breath they drew felt like an affront to the sanctity of this place, a haven twisted into a crypt.

"Something dwells here still," murmured Scáthach, her hands on the shaft of her spear, green eyes sharp as emeralds. Her chestnut hair, plaited in a long braid, grazed the scaled armour that sheathed her like a horned skin. Her voice held a timbre that resonated with the authority of the Lady of Earraghail, yet the empathy within it spoke of battles fought for more than just glory.

"Agreed," Naoise replied, his own hand upon the hilt of his sword, his senses stretched taut as bowstrings. He moved with the grace of a stag, every step deliberate, every sound catalogued. His black beard did little to hide the grim set of his jaw or the poetic sorrow that had etched itself into his features, the sorrow of a father torn from his ill child's bedside.

A turn in the passage revealed a grimmer aspect of the cave, bodies, or what remained of them, littered the uneven floor like macabre breadcrumbs. Each one a silent testament to the Fachan's insatiable appetite, their flesh yielded to time and the relentless gnawing of crabs and the unseen denizens of the deep.

"Manannán guard their souls on their journey to the House of Donn," Naoise muttered, his voice a low dirge for the lost. He knelt beside one of the less ravaged corpses, noting the terror forever sculpted on its waterlogged face. "These were not warriors," he said, the cadence of his speech a song of mourning. "They were fishermen, common folk."

"Then let us grant them vengeance," Scáthach intoned, steel in her words. She bowed her head momentarily in respect for the fallen, an unspoken oath passing between her and the spirits that clung to this desolate place.

"Vengeance and honour," Naoise echoed, standing once more. Together, they continued their descent into the cavern's depths, each step a solemn promise that retribution would be wrought in blood and iron, for justice, for bravery, for family, and for the sacred bonds that tied them to those they cherished.

Their journey deeper into the darkness was a palpable thing, a weight that pressed upon them with every corpse they passed, every inch they reclaimed from the abyss. It was a path of sorrow, a testament to the brutality of a creature that knew no kinship, only hunger.

And though the stench of death clawed at their nostrils and the cold seeped into their bones, Naoise and Scáthach pressed forward, undaunted. For beneath the layers of warrior and hunter, beneath the burdens of nobility and duty, beat hearts fuelled by the fervent flames of love and loyalty. And those flames would not be quenched until the beast that lurked in the watery shadows was vanquished.

The narrow passageway opened abruptly into a cavern of such vastness that Naoise and Scáthach paused at its threshold, momentarily taken aback. A grotto sprawled before them, an otherworldly domain where the laws of land yielded to those of water. Here, the sea's dominion was absolute, its surface an undulating mirror reflecting a spectral dance of light upon the jagged cave walls.

"Manannán's mantle," Naoise whispered, his voice a reverent hush amidst the eerie quietude, as if the god of the sea himself had woven a tapestry of liquid twilight within this hidden chamber.

Scáthach nodded, her eyes narrowed in focus. "Aye, but it is a beauty that belies danger."

The water shimmered with a luminescence that seemed to breathe life into the shadows, ghostly patterns that flickered and wavered like the souls of the dead, yearning for the touch of the living. It was a beauty born of darkness and depth, the murúch's allure, the siren that sang of mysteries untold and fates yet unwritten.

Their gazes locked, and in that glance passed a silent vow, an unyielding resolve to end the reign of terror cast by the beast they hunted. With a shared nod, they stepped forward, their presence an intrusion upon this sanctum of solitude.

As if summoned by their defiance, the silence ruptured with a roar that shook the very air around them. From the depths rose the Fachan, its monstrous form breaching the surface in a cascade of frothing waves. Its evil eye burned with malevolence, fixated upon the two warriors who dared challenge its sovereignty.

"By Lugh's spear," Scáthach cursed under her breath, readying the Gáe Bulg to strike.

Naoise drew in a steady breath, finding calm amidst the storm of his quickening pulse. He tossed his leather pack to the side and wedged his torch into a rocky crevasse, his bejewelled torc glinted in its flames. He raised his shield, his right hand taking a javelin, placing his finger through the leather tong and raising it over his head. His dark hair seemed to bristle with electric anticipation, his eyes mirroring the turbulence of the waters before him.

"Stand fast, Scáthach," he intoned, the lyrical timber of his battle-ready voice a stark contrast to the creature's guttural barks. "We strike as one."

"Until the end," she affirmed, her stance wide and ready, the horn-scaled armour hugging her form glinting with determination.

The Fachan surged forward, its sleek visage twisted in a grotesque parody of nature's design, its body an amalgam of flesh and nightmare. The battle commenced, a clash of wills and iron, a testament to the bravery that coursed through the veins of those bound by blood and honour. Together, Naoise and Scáthach moved as echoes of each other's intent, their weapons raised not simply for vengeance, but for the future of all who called Alba home.

Naoise's javelin, sleek and deadly, sliced through the dank air of the grotto, its whistle a sharp counterpoint to the thrumming rage of the beast before them. He watched, muscles coiled, as the projectile struck true, embedding itself deep within the matted hide of the Fachan. A roar, loud enough to shake loose ancient stalactites, reverberated off the cavern walls, sending ripples across the water's inky surface.

"Your aim is true, Naoise mac Uisneach," Scáthach called out, her voice steady despite the fury they faced. "Now watch your flank!"

The creature's single eye, a pool of abyssal hatred, fixed upon Naoise. With a vengeful whinny, it lunged out of the water, its flippers flailing with the might of ocean storms. Naoise sidestepped, narrowly avoiding the wrathful charge, his shield raised high. The impact against the wood and leather was a dull thud that echoed into the depths, the force behind it nearly wrenching his arm from its socket.

"Áine's grace!" he cursed, steadying himself on the slippery rocks.

Scáthach, her green eyes fierce and unyielding, leapt forward with the agility of a wildcat. She joined Naoise's side, the Gáe Bulg dancing in lethal arcs. They moved in concert, their dance one of death and defiance, when one attacked the other defended, with precision honed through countless battles. Their blades sang a duet of metallic hisses, slashing at the beast's exposed flesh, fighting not just for themselves, but for Aífe and all of kingdom of Earraghail.

As the creature reeled from their coordinated assault, it snapped viciously at Scáthach. Its teeth, sharp as the promise of revenge, sank into her armoured chest with a sickening crunch. A gasp escaped her lips as she felt the bite of the monster's venomous intent.

"Scáthach!" Naoise's cry cut through the chaos, his heart hammering against his ribs.

Her fingers spasmed, loosening their grip on the Gáe Bulg; the legendary spear clattered against stone, its bronze head glinting ominously as it came to rest mere feet away. The Fachan, seizing the moment of vulnerability, dragged her toward the water with relentless strength. Her body hit the surface, sending up a spray that caught the dim light, casting prismatic droplets around them like a shower of fleeting jewels.

"Manannán, protect her!" Naoise prayed under his breath, fear sharpening his resolve.

Scáthach's form vanished beneath the waves, the monstrous silhouette of the Fachan obscuring her from view. Desperation clawed at Naoise's chest, yet he knew that panic would serve no purpose. The bond they shared was forged in combat and trust; if anyone could emerge from the depths, it was the warrior daughter of Árd-Greimne.

"Fight, Scáthach," he murmured, his voice lost to the sound of churning waters. "Fight and return to the surface, so we may finish this together."

Naoise's sea grey eyes narrowed, the chill of the cavern pressing against his skin as he witnessed Scáthach's form disappear into the water's embrace, pulled by the monstrous Fachan. His breath turned to mist in the cold air, but his resolve burned hotter than the forges of Lugh. With a swift motion born from years of battles and skirmishes, Naoise sheathed his sword and grasped the second javelin, a fletched ash pole, five feet in length, with a leather throwing thong and with flared barbs that hungered for the blood of the beast.

"May you fly true," he whispered, invoking the precision of Lugh himself as he let the javelin sail through the dank air of the grotto. The missile hissed as it flew through the water, until it found its mark in the creature's hide, eliciting a roar that shook the very stones beneath his feet.

The monster convulsed in pain, the water around it frothing like a cauldron of Morrígan's fury. Then, with a surge of power that spoke of dark depths and untold strength, the Fachan dove deeper, taking Scáthach's struggling form with it into the abyss below.

Below the surface, Scáthach fought. Her hair became unbraided and fanned out around her in an underwater tempest, each strand a silent witness to her struggle. The creature's grip was iron; the pressure of the deep clawed at her senses, but she refused to yield. Within her, the spirit of the goddess Áine stirred, fierce as the red mare, sovereign as the summer sun.

With a surge of will that defied the crushing dark, she twisted in the creature's grasp. Her armour, scaled like the creatures of Manannán's realm, caught the light as she drove her thumb into the beast's only eye. It released her with a bellow of rage and pain, and Scáthach kicked upwards, her warrior's heart guiding her back toward the flickering light above.

She broke the surface, gasping for the air that tasted of salt and survival. "Naoise!" Her voice echoed, clear and commanding despite the ordeal. "The Gáe Bulg!"

On the shore, Naoise's fingers closed around the spear's spiralled shaft, the weapon thirsty for vengeance. He measured the distance, his body coiled like a spring, his eyes locking onto Scáthach's outstretched hand. With a grunt, he launched the Gáe Bulg through the air, its flight as sure as a kingfisher's dive.

Time seemed to slow as the spear flew, the intricate leather thong trailing behind it. Scáthach reached, her green eyes fixed on the incoming salvation. Her fingers clasped the weapon with the familiarity of countless hours of training, her grip unyielding.

"Árd-Greimne's blood runs strong!" Naoise exclaimed, pride swelling in his chest as he watched her ready the spear, her hands resolute against the oncoming tide of darkness.

The grotto trembled as Scáthach's fingers curled around the Gáe Bulg, its leather thong slipping over her fingers with practiced ease. She drew back the spear with her left hand, her right handing gripping the shaft tightly struggling with the tension of the loaded tong, every muscle in her body coiled like a snake. The Fachan reared before her, its slick hide glistening with the malign intent of the deep. Scáthach remained defiant, her chestnut hair plastered to her cheeks. With a warrior's cry that resonated off the ancient stone walls, she loosed the spear.

The Gáe Bulg became a blur, a streak of vengeance piercing through the water with such force that droplets sprayed into the air, catching the light in a spectral dance. It met the beast with a sound like the crack of thunder. The spearhead struck true, and on impact, seven barbs erupted outward, blossoming like a deadly flower. A grotesque hole burst in the creature's side, spilling dark ichor into the clear waters of the grotto.

A guttural roar filled the chamber as the Fachan thrashed, its monstrous form contorting in agony. As the life ebbed from its eye, a strange, dark mist began to seep from its wounds, swirling around the spear that had spelled its doom. The shadows twisted and writhed, seeking purchase in the world of the living but slowly dissipating, leaving behind only the echo of their malice.

Scáthach watched, her breaths heavy with exertion, as the last of the darkness vanished. It was a victory, yet the lingering unease told of greater threats lurking beyond the reach of her spear, a reminder that this was but one battle in a war unseen, fought in the shadowed corners of the world.

"Burn in Áillen's fires," she whispered, her voice steady despite the remnants of fear. By the water's edge, Naoise stood vigilant, his gaze scanning the depths from which the creature had come, knowing too well that the peace they had won was a fragile thing, and that the songs of their triumph would carry far beyond the confines of these ancient caves.

With the rush of battle over, Scáthach's body trembled as she struggled to stay afloat. Her breaths come in ragged gasps, her face contorted in agony as she fought to stay conscious. As she struggled to stay afloat, Naoise plunged into the water, his body disappearing beneath the surface before resurfacing with powerful strokes towards Scáthach, helping her back to the shore. The water glimmering in the torch light, a peaceful contrast to the recent chaos.

Naoise's hands, though steady in the heat of battle, now trembled with a healer's care as he knelt beside Scáthach on the rocky shore of the grotto. The warrior maid lay back against the cool stone, her chestnut hair splayed like a warrior's banner, her breaths ragged from exertion and the bite of the beast. He reached into his leather pack, retrieving the salves and bandages his mother had taught him to use, a lore not sung of in the mead halls, but no less vital.

"Be still, Scáthach," Naoise murmured, his sea grey eyes reflecting the concern etched into his brow. His fingers, calloused from sword hilt and sling, now worked gently to unbuckle her armour and cleanse her wounds, the scent of herbs and clean linen mixing with the brine of the cave air. He wrapped the bandage around her body with practiced precision, the white cloth stark against the dark bruises on her ribcage.

"Your hands wield kindness as deftly as they do a blade," Scáthach said, her voice laced with pain but also admiration. She watched Naoise, noting the tender dichotomy within him, a duality of might and mercy that she too harboured in the depths of her warrior soul.

"Your teaching saved us both this day," Naoise replied, securing the bandage with a knot. "It is only fitting that I tend to its preservation. Your ribs are broken."

"My horn armour is impenetrable," Scáthach replied through a grimace of pain.

"You are lucky that it is, otherwise that bite would have been cleaved you in two!" Naoise said, incredulous that Scáthach was still alive.

With her wounds bound, together they turned their attention to the fallen Fachan, its broken form washed onto the shore. Its once fearsome form lay still, the currents of dark magic that had animated it now vanquished. In silence, they acknowledged the gravity of what lay before them, their shared victory over darkness, and the unspoken knowledge that greater threats would emerge from the shadows in time.

Their gazes met, an unspoken understanding passing between them. Together, they approached the creature, the finality of their task lending weight to each step. "Let us finish this," Naoise said, pulling out the Gáe Bulg and handing the spear back to Scáthach, its barbs tearing away chunks of the creature's flesh.

Scáthach, her green eyes alight with the fires of justice and retribution, twisted the bronze spearhead, its barbs retracting. With a swift motion, born of countless battles and a heart unyielding, she severed the head of the Fachan. It fell with a splash, a grim trophy for King Árd-Greimne, a testament to their bravery and the strength of their alliance.

"May this victory bring peace to our lands," Scáthach declared, her words echoing through the cavern. Naoise nodded, his heart swelling with pride for their accomplishment and the bond forged in combat's crucible.

"Let us return this token of triumph to your father," he said, offering his hand to help her rise. "Together, we have quelled the darkness, and together, we shall carry its proof."

As they exited the grotto, the weight of the beast's head heavy between them, their steps were resolute, their spirits fortified by the knowledge that this day, at least, the gods had favoured them with victory.

The sail unfurled with a snap, catching the wind as Naoise steered their vessel through the churning waters, the green slime seemed now to have been washed away. Scáthach sat at the prow, her posture rigid in pain, her eyes scanning the horizon towards Dún Ad. The sea, vast and relentless beneath the burgeoning light of dawn, mirrored the tumult in their hearts.

"Swift as Manannán's horses, may we fly across these waves," Naoise murmured, casting a glance at the churning foam trailing in their wake. His hands gripped the rudder with the same sureness that had wielded sword and shield in the caverns' depths.

"And may Lugh's piercing gaze clear our path and hasten Aífe's healing," Scáthach replied, her voice barely rising above the roar of the sea. Her hair whipped about her face, the salt air mingling with the scent of battle still clinging to her scaled armour.

The grotto's darkness seemed to cling to their memories, but they forced their thoughts towards the light of hope. Neither spoke of the shadows that lingered at the edge of thought, the unspoken fears for what awaited upon their return. Their silence was filled instead with the creak of wood and the slap of waves against the leather hull.

Naoise's eyes held a storm of emotions, each as raw and fierce as the waves they coursed through. He let out a song, a lilting melody that rose above the din, weaving courage and resolve into the very air they breathed. It was a hymn to bravery, to the love that bound them to those they fought for.

Scáthach listened to the haunting notes, allowing the beauty of Naoise's voice to soothe the pain in her wound and fortify her spirit. She thought of Aífe, young and brave, her resilience a beacon that now guided them home.

"Her parent's strength flows in Aífe's veins," Scáthach said after a time, her words meant to bolster both their spirits. "She will stand tall again, and we shall be there to aid her rise."

"Indeed," Naoise agreed, his tone imbued with a healer's compassion. "And should the Dagda look kindly upon us, our actions this day will have preserved more than just one life."

Their course remained true as the sun lifted higher, its rays piercing the morning mist. The head of the Fachan lay wrapped in sailcloth at the bottom of the boat, a grim reminder of the cost of peace and the valour required to maintain it.

As Dún Ad's outline emerged from the fog, Naoise's heart quickened. They would soon face the aftermath of their quest, the healing of wounds and the restoration of balance. Yet within him stirred the knowledge that whatever trials awaited, they would face them united, as steadfast allies bound by the deepest respect and an unyielding sense of duty.

"Let us make haste," he called to Scáthach, his words cutting through the calm. "Our journey is not yet at its end."

"Nor shall it ever be," she replied, her green eyes reflecting a warrior's resolve. "For every ending births a new beginning."

With that, they sailed on, the coast drawing nearer with each passing moment, carrying with them the head of the beast, the weight of victory, and the fervent hope for a daughter's recovery.

Chapter 7

Aífe's Vision

Deirdre's fingers traced the outline of her daughter's fevered brow, a whisper-thin caress against the heat that raged beneath Aífe's skin. Each touch was a silent prayer, a mother's plea to the ancient gods who watched over their blood-steeped lands. Her voice, a murmur lost in the shadows of the room, was laced with the essence of hope, fragile as a spider's silk yet relentless in its quiet insistence.

"Rest now, my little one," she whispered, brushing a lock of golden hair from Aífe's brow. The girl stirred but did not wake, and Deirdre's hand lingered, seeking comfort in the soft warmth of her daughter's skin. The red scars on Aífe's leg, a stark reminder of the peril they had faced, seemed to pulse with an accusation, a testament to the dangers lurking beyond their sheltered haven. "Rest and let the healing spirits do their work." But beneath the steady thrum of her whispered comfort lay an undercurrent of fear, for the prophecy that had long ensnared her life now threatened to claim her child.

Along the wall of the crannóg, where the hearth's glow could barely reach, stood Ethniu, her hands moving with a deliberation born of countless seasons. The herbs in her grasp were but humble things, plucked from the embrace of the earth, yet in her aged fingers they were alchemy waiting to be wrought. As she crushed and mixed, her voice rose in a chant soft as the rustle of leaves, invoking the grace of Dian Cécht, god of healing, whose nurturing waters coaxed sickness from the infirm.

The druid's movements were a dance of precision and purpose; each step, each turn of her wrist, was a testament to years spent in communion with the rhythms of nature. The calm determination etched into her weathered face belied the urgency that charged the air, for in her wisdom she knew well the gravity of Aífe's plight.

"Ancestors of old, lend me your strength," Ethniu intoned, her voice carrying the weight of the sea and the steadfastness of the mountains. She did not waver, for her spirit was anchored deep in the bedrock of her beliefs, and her resolve to save Aífe shone as clear as the first rays of Lugh's dawn.

The tension in the crannóg was a living thing, thick as the peat smoke that clung to the rafters. Deirdre's heart pounded in her chest, drumbeat of fear that resonated through the small, shadowed space. Her eyes, deep pools of blue that once mirrored the calm skies above, now flickered with the light of torches, darting between Ethniu's stooped form and the still figure of Aífe.

Deirdre's hands, once steady as she wove her golden tapestries, now trembled like leaves in an autumn gale. They fluttered to her lips, then to the silver crescent at her throat, a memory of the time when she defied the druid's prophecy that had haunted her since birth.

Druid's Promise

Ethniu's chant weaved through the air, a melody older than the hills of Alba. As she applied the herbal poultice to Aífe's wounds, her fingers were deft and assured, coaxing life back into the pallid flesh. The druid's ancient brown eyes held a spark of the eternal, a testament to her bond with the land and its secrets.

In the silence that followed each verse of Ethniu's incantation, Deirdre's mind raced, chased by the spectre of the prophecy that had haunted her life, a vision of bloodshed and sorrow that had driven her into the wilderness, away from Conchobar's possessive grasp. Yet here, in this moment of helplessness, it was not the shadows of foretold tragedy that tightened her chest, but the very real dread that her daughter might slip beyond her reach.

"Please," she whispered to the gods, to Donn who governed life and death, "not my Aífe. Not my child."

Her thoughts cascaded like the streams of her homeland, tumbling over memories of Naoise's embrace, the laughter of his brothers, and the solemn promise she had made to herself, to shield her child from the cruel talons of fate. It was a vow etched into her soul, a fierce resolve that burned brighter even as hope's flame threatened to sputter out.

"Fight, little one," Deirdre murmured, her voice a fragile lifeline cast into the churning seas of uncertainty. "Your story is not yet sung."

As Ethniu worked, Deirdre's gaze lingered on the rise and fall of Aífe's chest, each breath a silent prayer to Manannán to guide her through the mists, back to the shores of the waking world. In the glow of the firelight, with the druid's whispered blessings wrapping around them like a cloak, mother and daughter stood at the crossroads of mortal will and divine whimsy, their fates intertwined with the ancient magic that pulsed beneath the soil of their beloved Éirinn.

Aífe's breaths, once shallow and rhythmic, now clawed their way out in ragged gasps that seemed to wrestle with the very air around her. Each heave of her small chest was an uneven staccato, a distressing counterpoint to the steady cadence of rain pattering against the thatched roof of the crannóg. Deirdre's hand, entwined with her daughter's, became a vice of fear as she willed the life within Aífe not to fade. The clamminess of the child's skin beneath her fingertips spoke of a body besieged, a stark contrast to the warmth that once radiated from her like the hearthfire of home.

"Stay with me, my darling" Deirdre implored, each word infused with desperation as if they alone could anchor Aífe's spirit. The venom, a malevolent intruder, tightened its grip with each passing moment, threatening to extinguish the vibrant flame of her young life.

Ethniu, her hands steady during the hours of her ministrations, halted her chant mid-verse. The druid's gaze lifted, locking with Deirdre's for a breathless instant, conveying an understanding that bridged the gap between mother's love and healer's wisdom. In that silent communion, words were unnecessary; both women recognized the precipice upon which Aífe teetered, the balance between this world and the Otherworld, where the Tuatha Dé whispered secrets just beyond mortal comprehension.

The weight of unvoiced fears settled heavy on Deirdre's shoulders, as heavy as the oaken door of the crannóg that kept the biting winds at bay. Yet within that shared glance with Ethniu, there was also a silent vow, a pact sealed by their joint vigil over the innocent caught in the crossfire of unseen battles. It was a testament to their collective resolve to defy the fickle threads of fate that sought to weave sorrow into the fabric of their lives once more.

Time seemed to stretch and warp within the confines of the crannóg, its fabric thinning as if reality itself were fraying at the edges. Deirdre hovered over Aífe, her daughter's life a fragile thread in the loom of existence, each laboured breath a knot that might unravel at any moment. The smoky air grew still, the crackling of the hearth's fire dimming to a hush, as though the elements themselves stood in reverence of the unfolding drama.

In that charged silence, an inexplicable change whispered through the room. It was not a sound, nor a visible sign, but an intangible altering of the world's essence. The shadows cast by the firelight seemed to dance with renewed fervour, and the scent of the healing herbs infused the air with a potency that spoke of ancient magics stirring.

Deirdre felt it in her marrow, an unspoken promise that wound its way through her spiralling fears, a harbinger of something momentous.

Then, as sudden as the onset of a summer storm, came the turning point. The walls of the crannóg seemed to breathe with newfound life, and outside, beneath the waxing moon, the echoes of a distant struggle reached their crescendo. It was there, in the collision of unseen forces, that the Fachan, a creature born of Manannán's realm, met its end, its death cry unheard yet felt by all.

At that precise instant, a soft blush crept upon Aífe's cheeks, the pallor of sickness giving way to the rosy glow of health. Her breathing, once a laborious fight against the venom's embrace, now flowed with the ease of a calm sea after a tempest's wrath. Witnessing the transformation, Deirdre's heart, so constricted by dread, swelled with an overwhelming tide of relief. She gathered Aífe into her arms, her embrace a bastion against the darkness they had both endured.

"Pulse of my heart," she wept, her tears cascading freely as gratitude mingled with her prayers to the gods, Macha for her nurturing spirit, Dian Cécht for his healing waters, even Morrígan, who in her capacity as a weaver of fate, may have stayed her ominous hand this night. Deirdre held her daughter close, Aífe's heart beating strong against her own, a symphony of life that sang sweeter than any bard's tale.

And in that moment, beneath the thatched roof where ancient spirits watched and the world held its breath, a mother's love triumphed over the remnants of malice, as hope rekindled like the first rays of dawn scattering the remnants of night's deepest gloom.

Ethniu stepped back, the flicker of torchlight casting shadows over her age-etched face. Her eyes, deep-set and brown as forest earth, observed the girl's revival with a profound sense of wonder nestled within their wisdom-worn folds. She had walked the path of guide and healer for more moons than the villagers could count, her hands channelling the very essence of the land, its healing herbs, its whispered incantations, its sacred rhythms. Now, as life bloomed anew in Aífe's cheeks, Ethniu felt the ancient currents of magic affirming her place in the tapestry of existence.

Her lips, which had been moving quietly in unceasing prayer to Áine for the young one's vigour, now curved into a small, satisfied smile. It was not pride that warmed her heart, it was fulfilment, a silent acknowledgment that she had stood as a conduit for forces greater than any mortal understanding. In her resolute calm, there was reverence for the unseen powers that coursed through their world and gratitude to Dagda's benevolent gaze, which may have tilted the balance this night.

Aífe's eyelids fluttered, ushering in the hesitant dawn of consciousness. Her gaze, once lost in fevered dreams, wavered beneath the weight of confusion before it began to clear like the morning mist dissipating under Lugh's golden chariot. Deirdre's gentle hands cradled her, guiding the tentative resurgence of strength as Aífe sought to rise, her movements a fragile dance between reliance and the soul-deep urge to reclaim autonomy.

"Mam?" The word was a mere breath, a delicate sound that seemed almost too tender for the air to bear.

"Shh, my heart," Deirdre murmured, steadying Aífe's shoulders with a touch both protective and empowering. "You're safe."

In the dim light of the crannóg, time seemed to stretch and pause, honouring the sacredness of a daughter pulled back from the brink, a mother's whispered prayers answered, and the quiet pride of a druid whose life's work was vindicated by the resilience of the human spirit intertwined with the mysteries of the old gods.

Aífe's breath steadied, the rhythm of life finding its familiar cadence within her once more. Her small hand sought Deirdre's, fingers twining with a grip that spoke volumes of her returning vigour.

"Mam," Aífe whispered again, her voice stronger now, carrying the weight of worlds unseen. "I dreamt of shadows and fire, of a harp whose music called forth flames that danced like living things."

Deirdre's heart caught at the mention of malevolent craft of Áillen, the mischievous god of fire. She leaned closer, her voice a hushed thread amidst the stillness. "Tell me, my child. What else did you see?"

"The flames... they were not just to destroy. They showed me visions." Aífe's eyes, reflecting the pale glow of the hearth, brimmed with wonder and an ancient knowing that seemed too vast for her tender years. "The first was beneath the sea, in a cavern of green light and stone. I saw Dad, and a warrior woman with hair like copper, fighting side by side against the monster that attacked me. When the creature fell, I felt something, an ancient energy surging through my body."

Deirdre drew in a breath, her chest tightening with awe and unease. "A vision of Naoise and Scáthach in the deeps," she murmured, more to herself than to the others.

"There was a white horse too," Aífe continued, her voice now quickening with the momentum of memory. "Galloping across the sea, its mane ablaze with stars. And man and woman, fierce and beautiful, riding on its back."

"Visions bestowed by the gods," Ethniu interjected softly, her presence near yet unobtrusive. Her eyes held the glint of moonlight on water, and she nodded slightly, acknowledging the sacred gift imparted to the young seer before them.

"Was there more, Aífe?" Deirdre questioned, her own curiosity mingling with apprehension.

"Only fragments," Aífe murmured, her gaze distant as if she traversed worlds beyond the crannóg's walls. "A raven circling overhead, a spear alight with the sun's fury, and a sea that whispered secrets in a language I almost understood."

"Symbols of our deities," Deirdre breathed, the realization dawning upon her like a revelation. "Morrígan, Lugh, Manannán... You have been touched by the divine."

"Perhaps it is a sign," Ethniu mused, her tone contemplative, "that Aífe is destined for a path intertwined with the gods, a conduit between this realm and theirs."

Deirdre turned toward Ethniu, their gazes locking in a moment laden with unspoken understanding. In the old druid's eyes, there was a recognition of the forces that had conspired to return Aífe from the clutches of death, and in Deirdre's, a gratitude that shimmered through her tears.

With care, Deirdre drew Aífe into her embrace, the warmth of her daughter's body a testament to the life that coursed anew within her. "My brave girl," she whispered, her words a benediction. "We will navigate this journey together."

Ethniu watched them, the lines of age and wisdom etched upon her face softening into a smile. There was much to ponder, many implications of Aífe's newfound sensitivity to the otherworldly. But for now, the crannóg was a sanctuary of reprieve, and hope had indeed returned to nestle in the heart of a mother who had known only fear for far too long.

"Rest now," Ethniu said, her voice a gentle decree. "For today, we have triumphed. Tomorrow, we shall see what fates the gods have woven for us."

And so, as the night deepened around them and the embers of the hearth glowed like dying stars, Deirdre held her daughter close, her heart filled with a cautious optimism that whispered of dawn's light on the horizon.

Deirdre brushed a stray lock of Aífe's hair from her forehead, the faint thrum of life beneath her fingertips a fragile promise in the stillness of the crannóg. The fire had sunk to coals, casting an undulating dance of shadows upon the walls, and through the wattle and daub, the night whispered of things unseen.

"Mam," Aífe murmured, her voice a ghostly echo of its former strength, "the dreams... they spoke of tempests and turmoil, of paths entwined with thorns and blood."

Deirdre's heart clenched within her chest, the precarious joy she felt now tinged with the bitter tang of foreboding. This was no mere fevered rambling; it was a glimpse into the tapestry of fate that the gods themselves wove in secret.

"Sleep, child," Deirdre soothed, though her own mind raced with thoughts of prophecies and portents. "We shall brave whatever storms may come, together."

Aífe's brow furrowed, even as her eyelids fluttered closed, succumbing to the deep embrace of sleep once more. But the air around them seemed charged, as if the very essence of Aífe's visions lingered, waiting to be born into reality.

Ethniu, too, sensed the shift, the undercurrent of change that ran as deep as the roots of the ancient oaks. She moved to the doorway, peering out into the darkness where the realm of man met the mysteries of the gods. The druid knew that the struggle they had faced this night was but the first of many; for the gods delighted in weaving complexity into the lives of mortals.

"Deirdre," Ethniu called softly over her shoulder, her gaze fixed across the loch, on the distant hills shrouded in mist, "the threads of destiny are not easily unravelled. This night's victory will echo in the halls of kings and the whispers of the Otherworld."

Deirdre joined Ethniu at the door, her eyes drawn to the horizon where dawn would soon break. In the east, the earliest hint of light teased the edge of night, a pale harbinger of the day to come. It promised a new beginning, yet also cast long shadows, shadows that might hide friend or foe, blessing or curse.

"Let them come," Deirdre said, her voice steady despite the uncertainty that clawed at her spirit. "We are the blood of Éirinn, the kin of Macha and the children of prophecy. Our loyalty to each other is our strongest shield, our will to prevail our sharpest spear."

"Indeed," Ethniu replied, her eyes reflecting the first glimmer of dawn's light. "But remember, Deirdre, that the path of bravery often leads through peril, and the flame of revenge can sear the hands that wield it. Yours and Aífe's visions herald trials ahead, not just for her, but for all of us."

A rooster crowed in the distance, its call a declaration that the night had ended, but as Deirdre gazed upon her slumbering child, she understood that their true challenge was just beginning. What lay ahead was a journey that would test the bonds of family and loyalty, a path fraught with the machinations of both mortal ambition and divine intrigue. Deirdre wrapped her cloak tight around her shoulders. The tapestry of their lives was complex, woven with threads of love, vengeance, and the inscrutable will of the gods. And though the dawn promised light, it was the shadows of the future that beckoned them onward.

Chapter 8

Celebrations in Dún Ad

The currach glided into the harbour of Dún Ad, its leather-clad hull slicing through the still waters with a hushed reverence. Naoise's muscles ached from the relentless rowing, but his heart was alight with victory. Beside him, Scáthach sat poised as ever, her green eyes reflecting the myriad hues of the sea, a warrior's gaze never betraying the fatigue that clawed at her chest.

As they reached the pebbled shore, the villagers emerged like a tide from their homes and workplaces, their faces etched with hope and curiosity. They clustered along the harbour, their eager voices blending together in a chorus of anticipation.

"Tell us," they clamoured, "has the beast fallen?"

Naoise stepped onto the wooden wharf, the boards creaked under his boots as he walked. He looked upon the assembly, allowing a smile to curve his lips, the gesture carrying the weight of their triumph.

"By the grace of Lugh's spear," Naoise proclaimed, his voice rich with pride, "the Fachan will no longer haunt the shores of Alba."

A cheer rose from the villagers, their relief palpable as it resonated through the air. The shadow of fear, which had loomed over them, was now lifted, dissolved by the light of their courage and determination.

In the doorway of the crannóg, Deirdre stood frozen for a moment, her blue eyes wide as they saw Naoise and Scáthach. The two warriors standing tall among the crowd. Her heart thundered against her ribs, echoing the drumbeat of a long-awaited reunion. Then, as if released from an enchantment, she surged forward, her golden tresses streaming behind her like the banners of returning heroes.

"Naoise!" she cried, her voice a melody that soared above the din.

Their embrace was a fortress built from the threads of love and longing, strong enough to withstand the torrents of fate. Naoise enfolded Deirdre within his arms, feeling the tremble of her body against his own, a tremor not of frailty, but of overwhelming emotion.

"Dearest, I missed you so," he whispered into her hair, inhaling the scent of meadows and the warmth of sunlit days spent in her company, "how fares our little warrior?"

"Aífe," she pulled back just enough to gaze into his eyes, her own shimmering with tears and joy, "she's recovering. Her fever has broken, and her wounds are mending."

"Thank the Dagda," Naoise breathed out in fervent relief, a prayer of gratitude to the father of all gods for his daughter's resilience. His chest swelled with a newfound peace, for in Deirdre's words lay the promise of a future free from the shadow of dread that had once threatened to engulf them all.

"Come," Deirdre said, her hand clasping his, "let us go to her. She's been asking for you."

"I will take my leave," Scáthach informed them both. "I must tell my father and daughter about our triumph."

Naoise placed his hand on her shoulder as a gesture of gratitude and shook her hand. "Thank you for all that you've done," he expressed sincerely.

Scáthach the turned and made her way towards the winding path that led to the top of the hill.

Together, Deirdre and Naoise crossed the threshold of the crannóg, leaving behind the echoes of a battle hard-won and stepping into the tender embrace of family reunited.

"Dad," Aífe's joyful voice echoed through the room, "did you defeat the monster?"

"We won, my darling," Naoise replied with a smile, "it was a tough battle, but Scáthach used her enchanted spear to vanquish the monster."

"A magic spear?" Aífe exclaimed in wonder.

"Yes, a magic spear," he said as he embraced his daughter. "I am overjoyed that you are healing well and the shadow of the Fachan has passed."

* * *

The air of Dún Ad shimmered with a jubilance that seemed to rise from the earth itself, as if the very soil rejoiced at the news of the Fachan's demise. Outside Ethniu's crannóg laughter rippled through the crowd like a brook freed from winter's grasp, and the thrum of harps, the whistle of pipes and the beats of bodhráns set hearts aflame with rhythm. Lads and lasses, emboldened by triumph, joined hands in circles, their feet drumming out a dance as ancient as the hills that cradled their village.

Naoise, standing tall amidst the revelry, felt a kinship with the mirth that enveloped him. The music, he noted, carried the wildness of the wind through Macha's mane, and the dancers mirrored the lively sparks of Aengus' youthful vigour. It was a scene etched in the hues of life itself, painted with the brushstrokes of communal relief and gratitude.

As the celebration swelled, two figures emerged from behind the harbour wall, their shadows lengthening with the setting sun's benediction. Ardan, his brown hair tousled and eyes alight with merriment, led the way, his voice carrying over the din. "Naoise!"

Ainnle followed close behind, his gaze scanning the crowd until it found the familiar faces etched into his heart. Though shyer in demeanor than his twin, a smile carved a path across Ainnle's features, a silent testament to the bond shared within Clan Uisneach.

"Brothers!" Naoise called out, his own smile a beacon as they approached. They rushed forward, arms open, embracing each other in a tangle of limbs that bespoke of unity reforged in the crucible of adversity.

"By Lugh's spear, you've returned!" Naoise exclaimed, the joy of reunion igniting his words with warmth.

Ardan clapped him on the back, his laughter an echo of their childhood escapades. "And miss a feast worthy of the Dagda himself? Never," he quipped, his blue eyes dancing with unspoken tales of their search.

"How did your hunt fare," Naoise inquired of his brothers.

Ainnle replied, "We sailed south for three days, scouring the waters and questioning the fisherfolk for any signs of the elusive creature."

Ardan chimed in, "But on the fourth day, news of your triumph had reached us, so we turned back towards Dún Ad with the wind in our sails."

"Your bravery will be sung by bards, Naoise," Ainnle added, his tone earnest, a reflection of the respect he held for his elder brother.

"Ah, but the song is not mine alone," Naoise said, gesturing to the villagers who now surrounded them, each face a verse in the ballad of their survival. "It belongs to all who dare to stand against the dark tide."

They stood there, united in their victory, as the sounds of celebration continued to swell around them. Instruments played, and voices rose in chorus, a symphony dedicated to those who had faced the abyss and returned to tell the tale. Together, under the canopy of twilight, Clan Uisneach embodied the very essence of home, a harbour in the storm, where kinship and loyalty anchored the soul.

* * *

Torches flickered in their sconces along the wooden carvings of the grand hall, casting long shadows over the faces of nobles and warriors gathered in King Árd-Greimne's court. The air was heavy with the scent of peatsmoke and the quiet murmur of anticipation. At the high table, the king sat like a sentinel, his eyes fixed on the entrance where Scáthach now stood poised to make her presentation.

Clad in her armour that sparkled like fish scales under the torchlight, Scáthach advanced down the aisle with measured steps, each footfall echoing through the hushed chamber. In her hands, she carried the grisly trophy of victory, a bloody sailcloth whose contents promised to tip the balance between fear and security within the realm.

As she reached the centre of the hall, a silent command from the king invited her forward. His gaze upon Scáthach bore the weight of a king's detachment and a father's love for his daughter. She ascended the dais with the dignity of one who has walked through the shadow of death and emerged unscathed. Her green eyes, reflecting the fire around her, sought out Naoise, who awaited at the end aisle next to the great doors. He stood solemn, his raven locks and snow-white skin a stark contrast against the sea of colours surrounding him.

"King Árd-Greimne, noble lords, and valiant warriors of this court," Scáthach began, her voice resonating with an authority softened by humility. "We gather here not to revel in the horrors of fear but to acknowledge the deliverance from a peril that threatened to consume us all, the Fachan, the beast of myth and terror has been destroyed."

She undid the twine that held the cloth closed and tipped its content onto the polished stone before the king, revealing the severed head of the monstrous creature. A collective intake of breath filled the room; it was the visage of nightmares made flesh, now lifeless and defeated.

"Let it be known that this victory would not have been possible without the bravery and skill of

Naoise mac Uisneach, Prince of Éirinn," Scáthach continued, turning to face the assembly, her hand beckoning Naoise to come forward. "His strength of arm and purity of heart turned the tide of battle. His song will echo in our lands, a melody of courage that overcame the darkness."

A swell of respect washed over the crowd, as the gathered nobility and warriors turned their gaze upon Naoise. His cheeks, usually tinged with rosy vitality, bore a humble flush. Yet, despite the reverence directed at him, his grey eyes remained steadfast, reflecting a knowing that such recognition was not his alone to bear.

"Scáthach speaks too generously," Naoise replied, his lyrical voice carrying across the hall with an earnestness that held the audience captive. "The beast was vanquished by the unity and resolve of Clan Uisneach and the people of Éarraghail. It was together we stood, and by the favour of the gods, it was together we triumphed."

In that moment, the greatness of the exiles shone clear for all to see, their honour untarnished by exile, their valour immortalized by deeds, and their loyalty to each other unbreakable. The court erupted into a chorus of cheers and applause, reverberating off the ancient walls, an ode to the indomitable spirit that had returned home not only in body but in glory.

Amidst the murmurs of admiration and the lingering echo of cheers, King Árd-Greimne rose from his throne, a commanding presence at the head of the grand hall. The assembly fell into respectful silence as he stood, his regal bearing underscored by the intricate embroidery of his tunic that shimmered like the surface of a calm sea under the flickering torchlight.

His face, usually an inscrutable mask of kingly authority, broke into a broad, genuine smile, a rare sight that spoke volumes of the moment's significance. He surveyed those gathered before him, his eyes eventually settling on Naoise, who stood with quiet dignity among his kin.

"Brave warriors of Clan Uisneach," he began, his voice resonant and clear, "this day shall be etched in the annals of our realm as one of triumph over darkness. You came to my lands as wayfarers in exile, but now you are our saviours, your deeds a testament to the strength and courage of your bloodline."

Naoise felt the weight of the king's gaze, a silent acknowledgment of their shared bond as men who valued love and honour above all else.

"Your actions have ensured the safety and prosperity of my people, and such valour merits a reward befitting its rarity." King Árd-Greimne's announcement hung in the air, laden with promise. A hush of anticipation enveloped the hall, as if the very stones themselves awaited the king's next words.

"By my decree, let it be known that Clan Uisneach shall henceforth hold dominion over the valley of Loch Eite. This land, rich and fertile, shall belong to you and your descendants, in recognition of the blood and bravery you have so freely given."

A collective gasp rippled through the crowd, a wave of astonishment that crested and broke into a fervent murmur. It was a gift beyond expectation, a bountiful offering that would root the exiles firmly into the soil of Alba. In granting them this land, the king not only rewarded their heroism but acknowledged their place within the fold of his kingdom.

Naoise, taken aback by the magnitude of the proclamation, felt the ground beneath him grow more solid, as though the earth itself recognized the gravity of the gesture. A sense of belonging unfurled within him, a tether to the land that had been forged in battle and now sealed by royal edict.

His family, standing alongside him, shared glances that spoke of relief and newfound hope. This was the turning point they had dared not dream of, a chance to build a future, to cultivate a life rich with the same tenacity that had brought them victory.

King Árd-Greimne's smile held a touch of reverence as he regarded the faces of the exiles, seeing in them the reflection of his realm's enduring spirit. "Let it be known," he continued, "that the loyalty and courage of Clan Uisneach shall forever be honoured in Alba. Today, justice has been served, bravery rewarded, and a family welcomed home."

The hall erupted once more, this time in jubilation, as the reality of the king's words settled upon the hearts of all present. For Naoise and his kin, the path forward was now clear, illuminated by the light of opportunity and the warmth of a homeland embraced.

In the shadowed embrace of King Árd-Greimne's grand hall, Scáthach's keen eyes traced the lines of incredulity etched upon her companions' faces. Naoise stood as the embodiment of their astonishment, his mouth slightly agape, the wind-weathered furrows of his brow softened by the king's pronouncement. The weight of exile, long carried upon their shoulders, seemed to lift and scatter like ash in a strong wind.

"Land," he murmured, his voice a quiet echo of disbelief. "A place we can finally call home."

Ardan, usually the first to voice scepticism, simply nodded, his face alight with dawning realization. Ainnle, ever stoic, allowed the edges of his lips to curl into a smile that reached his eyes, a rare expression of pure joy. The villagers clustered around them, their gazes warm with acceptance, a tapestry of shared triumph woven through every glance and gesture.

"Alba is your home now," Scáthach whispered, her warrior's heart uncharacteristically full. A sense of permanence settled among them, a collective sigh of relief breathed into the very stones of the hall. They were no longer wanderers tethered to the whims of fate; they had become sowers of their own destiny, in soil rich with promise.

The clangour of celebration called them forth from the reverie of their newfound fortune. The exiles raised their cups to the crowd and were met with a cacophony of jubilation. Tables groaned under the weight of roasted meats, freshly baked bread, and fruits glistening with honeyed glaze. Earthenware pitchers brimmed with ale and mead, the golden liquid catching the firelight that danced on the walls in flickering patterns.

Musicians strummed harps and thrummed bodhráns, their melodies weaving with the lilting voices of bards recounting tales both ancient and new. Laughter mingled with music, creating an atmosphere that pulsed with life, the heartbeat of a community united in revelry.

Naoise found himself swept along by the tide of merriment, his arm raised in salute to villagers who approached with wide grins and tankards raised high. He clinked his drink against theirs, the sound resonating with the promise of enduring kinship.

"Sláinte!" they cheered, voices raised over the din of festivity.

"Sláinte," he echoed, warmth blooming in his chest, not from the mead but from the knowledge that here, amidst the clatter of feasting and the symphony of joy, lay the foundation of home, a place where Clan Uisneach could forge a future sculpted by their own hands, beneath the watchful eyes of the gods as old and timeless as the rolling hills of Alba.

Meanwhile, Aífe's laughter rang clear as she regaled her uncles with the tale of her recovery. The white linen cloth on her leg caught the light as she animatedly retraced her steps from peril to perseverance.

"Next time I will slay the beast myself," she declared proudly, her voice carrying the vigour of one who had faced darkness and emerged emboldened.

Her uncles listened with rapt attention, pride swelling in their chests as they witnessed the young girl's burgeoning warrior spirit, tempered by trials and triumphs alike.

"Your courage honours us all, Aífe," Ardan said, his eyes alight with admiration.

"Indeed," added Ainnle, his smile broad and sincere. "You are the very essence of Clan Uisneach, undaunted, unyielding. But tell me truly, how did you recover so quickly? When we left, you could hardly breathe, and now... it is as though the beast left no mark upon you."

Aífe's smile softened, a flicker of memory passing across her face. "Ethniu thinks it was the Fachan itself that held me bound, its foul magic clinging to my spirit even after I escaped the water.

But when it was slain, the grip it had on me was broken. As its life ended, so too did its curse."

She glanced at the linen on her leg, her fingers brushing it absently. "The fever left me that very night, as though a shadow lifted from my soul. Ethniu said it was rare, but not unheard of, when a creature of dark power dies, its enchantments die with it."

Ardan's brow furrowed thoughtfully. "Then it was more than just a wound. It was a tether."

Aífe nodded. "A tether of fear and poison. But it is gone now. I feel it. I am free."

The firelight danced in her eyes, and her voice held no trace of doubt. Her uncles exchanged glances, a deepened respect settling between them, not only for her survival, but for the quiet wisdom she had earned through pain and peril.

"You are more than a warrior in the making," Ainnle said softly. "You are touched by the old magic, Aífe. May it always serve you well."

Amidst the revelry, Naoise's gaze found Deirdre's. A silent understanding passed between them, a wordless invitation to steal away from the exuberance that filled the air. They slipped through the throng of bodies, their hands finding each other's as they retreated into the quieter antechamber where shadows flickered along the walls.

"Look at them," Deirdre murmured, her moist eyes reflecting the glow of a nearby brazier, revealing the sadness in her smiling face. "Their spirits are as high as the night is deep."

"Indeed," replied Naoise, his voice a low hum that vibrated with the resonance of the bodhráns. "Our victory has lit a fire in their hearts, one that not even the chill winds of Alba can snuff out."

"What troubles you, my love?" Naoise asked with concern. "Is this not all we have ever wanted? A place of our own free from the grasp of Ulaid?"

"It is nothing," Deirdre said as she leaned her head against his shoulder, her golden hair spilling over the coarse fabric of his tunic like a cascade of sunlight. "The life we've always dreamt of, it begins here, with these people, in this land."

Naoise wrapped an arm around her, drawing her closer. "Together," he whispered, "we'll write our own tale, one of love and home, a story sung through the ages."

Their moment was a sanctuary, a private reprieve suffused with the weight of shared dreams and the delicate strength of hope.

Before the conversation could blossom further, Scáthach approached, her armour glinting like the scales of a fearsome leviathan from the depths of Manannán's domain. She laid a firm hand on Naoise's shoulder, her emerald eyes sparking with purpose.

"Come, Naoise," she beckoned. "Let us gift our people a song, a melody to mark our triumph and bind their hearts to ours."

Naoise nodded, offering Deirdre a parting kiss upon her brow before rising to join Scáthach. Together, they stood before the gathered crowd, their voices harmonizing to weave a ballad of valour and victory that soared above the din, entwining with the very essence of the hall.

As the final notes faded into the warmth of the night, a hush fell upon the assembly. In that stillness, a sense of hope and renewal blossomed like the first shoots of spring piercing winter's thaw. Each soul in attendance felt the palpable presence of a new dawn, the dawning of an era in which the exiles would no longer wander but would root themselves deeply into the fertile soil of Alba.

The smiles that graced the faces of Clan Uisneach spoke of more than mere happiness, they were emblems of the security and belonging that had eluded them for so long. Here, in this great hall under King Árd-Greimne's benevolent gaze, they glimpsed the contours of a future woven from the threads of their resilience and unity.

With songs still echoing in their hearts, they turned their eyes toward the horizon, where challenges awaited, veiled by the promise of adventures yet to come. In Alba, among friends and newfound kin, they would carve out their destiny, guided by the ancient gods and bound by the unshakeable ties of family and loyalty.

Chapter 9

Echoes from Emain Macha

The Lughnasadh feast unfurled beneath the high-vaulted red beams of the great roundhouse of Cróeb Ruad, a tapestry of jubilation woven with the threads of laughter and the hum of myriad conversations. The air was thick with the scent of roasting beef and pork, mingling with the earthy aroma of ale as it flowed freely among the gathering. Princes and nobles adorned in their finery, warriors marked by the glory of scars, and common folk dressed in their festive best, all came together to honour the sun god Lugh and his bountiful harvest.

Upon the central dais, on his throne at the feet of the monumental carving of the goddess Macha, sat King Conchobar mac Nessa. His fair hair, now streaked with the wisdom of grey, caught the flickering light of the torches. To his left sat Queen Mugain, her gaze regal and her bearing majestic. On the king's right hand sat the druid Cathbad, draped in white robes that symbolised the mastery of his ancient order, lent a silent strength to his son's side.

Seated below the dais, resplendent in his lavish silk tunic, was Éogan mac Durthacht, King of Fernmag. At his side Queen Findige appeared distant and uninterested. Their daughter, the beautiful Princess Lendabair sat between her children, Laidis and Uaithne, and her husband,

Conall mac Amargin, the valiant captain of the Red Branch warriors, golden and fierce as the sun god Lugh. Conall Cernach, they donned him, Conall the Victorious, for it is said that he never lost a fight. The family were a vision of royalty, exuding power and grace.

Across the hall, beside the great silver cauldron, the Ol nGuala, stood the towering sons of Róich, Fergus and Súaltam. They satisfied their thirst and observed the festivities with their commanding presence.

Feasting nearby were the young princes of Ulaid. Fiachna mac Fedelm, sat with his friend Illann mac Fergus. Twins in all but blood, they were both celebrating their birthdays today. Next to them were Follomain mac Mugain, the youngest son of Conchobar, and the inseparable duo, Lugaid mac Clothru and Sétanta mac Súaltam.

Nestled in a quiet side chamber far away from the dais, sat the Ollam Fedlimid mac Daill. Gathered around him were a curious crowd, men, women, and children, all eager for another tale of lore. Standing at the edge of the gathering, arms folded across his broad chest, was Dáire mac Fedlimid. He bore his father's sharp features, but where the ollam was draped in the robes of a scholar, Dáire wore the proud red cloak of the Red Branch warriors. His expression was impassive, though his keen eyes betrayed a watchful scepticism.

Druid's Promise

"Ah, come closer to the fire, and let me tell ye a tale of kings and warriors, of cunning and courage, of Ulaid's rise to glory," Fedlimid said as he glanced over to the giant brothers drinking by the cauldron. .

"Long ago, before ever a single king ruled over the land of Ulaid, it was two kingdoms that stood apart, their rulers each claiming right over the green hills and shadowed glens. But then came Ross Ruad, the Red Giant, a man of great strength and greater wisdom. He was not alone, for at his side stood his two brothers, Cathbad the druid, a master of lore and magic, and Cairbre the Red Hand, a fierce warrior whose name struck fear into the hearts of his foes. Together, the three brothers fought to unite the thrones of Ulaid, each lending his gift to the forging of a single realm.

With a firm hand and a keen mind, Ross Ruad battled his enemies wielding his great sword Caladbolg, which when swung left a rainbow in its wake. He did what none before him had done, he joined the two warring lands into one. And seeing the heart of Ulaid's power, he set his throne at Emain Macha, the jewel of the north.

There, the brothers built three great roundhouses. Ross raised Cróeb Ruad, the sacred hall in which we gather. Cathbad raised the Téite Brecc, a place of wisdom and recovery. Cairbre raised Cróeb Derg, to hold the spoils of their victories.

But they were not yet done, they founded the Red Branch warriors, a company of the boldest champions, bound by honour and skill. And with the strength of the Red Branch at their backs the brothers marched to Teamhair and where Ross Ruad claimed the throne of the High-King of Éirinn.

As High-King, Ross took wives from the north and from the south. Mágach, daughter of Aengus Óg and Róich, daughter of Fergus mac Léti, and had four sons Fachtna, Cet, Fergus, and Súaltam. For many a year he ruled, his reign long and prosperous, and when his time came, he left this world in peace, his task well done," Fedlimid's voice was a symphony of melodies and inflections, his bright blue eyes sparked with the energy and wisdom of a seasoned storyteller.

"Now, his son Fachtna Fáthach, took the throne as High-King of Éirinn. Wise and just he was, like his father before him. The kingship of Ulaid passed to Ross' cousin, Eochaid Sálbuide, known far and wide as Yellow-Heel. A strong ruler he was, but fate had its own plans, and his name is oft remembered not for his deeds alone, but for his daughter Nessa, mother to one who would shape Ulaid's destiny.

When war rose between the High-Kings, Eochaid and Cet stood with Fachtna, their swords lifted high against the enduring Eochu Feidlech, the rival who sought to claim the throne of Éirinn. But alas, the gods wove a different thread, and at the Battle of Leitir Ruadh, Cet turned against his brother. Yellow-Heel and Fachtna fell, their blood staining the earth they fought to defend." His words swirled and twirled around the tall red pillars of the hall, captivating his audience.

"And so the people turned to the eldest living son of Ross Ruad, Fergus mac Róich, a towering warrior of great renown, and made him the king of Ulaid. But Fergus was a man ruled by passion as much as by wisdom, and his heart burned for Nessa, daughter of the fallen king. Yet Nessa was no fool, she knew well the ways of men and the workings of power. 'I will be your wife,' she told him, 'but only if my son Conchobar sits the throne for one year. So that his sons, will have king's blood.'" Fedlimid narrated, as his light brown hair shimmered in the glow of the fire.

"Now, Fergus laughed at this, thinking no harm in it. For what was a year to a man of his strength? The nobles of Ulaid, too, nodded, believing a boy of seven years would be king in name only. But Nessa was a woman of deep cunning, and Conchobar, son of the druid Cathbad, was no ordinary child. With his mother's wit and his father's wisdom, he ruled so well, so justly, that when the year was done, the people would have none but him. And so, Fergus, who had once been king, stepped aside, not in anger, but in loyalty, for he saw the greatness in the boy's rule. He swore fealty to Conchobar and stood ever at his side, as both warrior and guide.

Fergus had a great love for women, and when Nessa passed he took no new wife. Instead he shared his bed with many of the woman of Ulaid, fathering many sons.

And in time, Fergus took to his hearth Cormac, the eldest son of Conchobar, and many more sons of kings, to foster and train in the arts of warfare. But those are tales for another night," his voice resonated throughout the hall he reached the climax of his tale.

"Now, drink deep and remember well, for the land of Ulaid was not built by swords alone, but by wit, by will, and by the hands of those who knew how to hold both power and honour in balance." Fedlimid said as he raised his cup and emptied it.

His audience clapped and cheered, but Dáire merely exhaled through his nose, unimpressed. Before his father could bask in the admiration, King Conchobar rose, his voice cutting through the din with the ease of a blade parting silk. "On this night of Lughnasadh, let it be known that the floor is open," he declared, his piercing blue eyes sweeping across those gathered. "As per our tradition at this harvest feast, I invite you to share your hearts' yearnings. I vow to Lugh to fulfil them, if it is within my power."

The crowd fell silent, anticipation crackling in the air like the embers of the bonfire on the great Mound of Macha outside, where the blessing of the gods of the sun and the moon was sought for fertility and abundance. It was a moment poised on the edge of revelation, where the unspoken could manifest into reality.

Amidst the sea of faces, a group of young warriors emerged, their spirits alight with purpose.

At their head was Cormac mac Clothru, with dark curly hair yet whose noble mien bore resemblance to the king yet softened by an undercurrent of empathy.

With each step he took toward the dais, murmurs undulated through the crowd, a wave of surprise that crested at his audacity and charismatic poise.

"Father, my king, and esteemed company," Cormac began, his voice steady as the roots of an oak. "We have heard tales from traders from Alba, songs of valour about the exiles, Deirdre and Naoise. It is told that Naoise, alongside the warrior maid Scáthach, has claimed victory over the Fachan, the vile water horse, whose terror ruled the waves. And as a reward for this heroic deed King Árd-Greimne has gifted Clan Uisneach the lands of Loch Eite."

His words hung in the air, an invocation that summoned images of clashing iron and triumphant courage. The tale was no mere feat; it was legend blooming from the lips of this young warrior. Eyes wide with wonder and whispers clothed in disbelief, the assembly could not help but be ensnared by the anticipation of Cormac's request.

"Is not the strength of Éirinn measured by the mettle of its kin?" Cormac pressed on, his voice a clarion call amidst the rising tide of unease. "Shall we let old auguries rule our fate, or shall we stand united, with Naoise's sword arm and Deirdre's foresight as our allies? It is time for Clan Uisneach to return home."

For it was not just a recount of heroism he offered them, but a plea, a call to embrace those who had been lost to exile, to strengthen the bonds of Éirinn with the return of its estranged children. And in this moment, amidst the revelry of Lughnasadh, the feast became a crucible for the hope of what was to come, a story of justice, bravery, and the complex weave of family loyalty that held the fate of a kingdom in its grasp.

A hush fell upon the great hall of Cróeb Ruad, as Cormac's declaration swirled among the gathered throng like a leaf caught in a tempest. Fedlimid shifted uncomfortably on his stool, taken aback by the unexpected request. Among the nobles and commoners alike, there were those whose faces brightened at the mention of Deirdre and Naoise, their hearts buoyed by tales of valour from across the sea. They nodded, their spirits kin with the young warriors' call for unity and strength, envisioning the exiles not as pariahs but as prodigal heroes returning to home.

Yet not all shared this fervour. A murmur of dissent threaded through the crowd, a tapestry of caution stitched by wary glances. Eyes flittered to King Conchobar, seeking a hint of his mind's bearing, but found none. Whispers passed from ear to ear, recounting the prophecy that had cast a shadow over Deirdre's life, the promise of beauty and doom intertwined. Dáire set his jaw, he knew well the burden his sister's name carried. The air grew taut with tension, each breath heavy with the weight of legends and fears long harboured.

King Conchobar remained as stone, his features a mask of sovereignty chiselled from the bedrock of his realm. Within the silence of his gaze, a war raged, an internal clash between the fires of his people's yearning and the ice of foretold calamity. The scales of destiny quivered under the weight of these opposing forces, waiting for the hand of his judgment to tip the balance.

At last, the king rose. His towering form cast a long shadow over the high table, the flickering torchlight unable to pierce the enigma of his countenance. The assembly watched, as if ensnared in some otherworldly rite, as Conchobar leaned over to the venerable Cathbad, his father and mystic seer, who sat alongside the king.

"Father," the king's voice finally broke the stillness, not with the boom of command, but with the gravity of mountains shifting. "Walk with me to my chambers. We have much to consider."

Cathbad rose, his staff tapping against the wooden dais in measured beats that seemed to echo the throbbing pulse of the world itself. Their departure was a procession marked by unspoken rituals, leaving the great hall of Cróeb Ruad simmering with anticipation and dread, for within those private chambers, the threads of fate would be unravelled and rewoven, guiding the course of a kingdom on the brink of legend.

The heavy oaken door to Conchobar's chambers thudded shut with a finality that seemed to swallow the merriment of the feast beyond. The king's private sanctum was a world apart, shrouded in tapestries and shadows, save for the crackle of the hearth fire that cast an otherworldly glow upon the room's wooden walls.

Cathbad produced a leather satchel from the hidden folds of his robes and emptied its contents on the table in centre of the chamber. He sorted through the sacred relics, raven bones etched with cryptic ogham, crystals that pulsed with the earth's deep magic, until he found what he was looking for, clay pots of dried mistletoe leaves drawn from the sacred oak trees. The air grew thick with musk as the druid added the leaves to the pot of water hanging over the fire, his hands trembling ever so slightly, not with age, but with the gravity of the divination he was about to perform.

"O Morrígan," Cathbad intoned, his voice a haunting melody that seemed to call forth spirits from the smoke, "harbinger of war and fate, lend me sight beyond the veil."

Conchobar watched, his fair hair flickering like captured flame in the half-light, his muscular form taut with anticipation. He remained still, a statue amongst the ephemeral dance of shadow and light, his sharp eyes fixed on Cathbad's every move.

The druid emptied the water upon the ground, and the chamber fell into a silence so profound it bordered on the sacred. Cathbad examined the remaining leaves, their shapes and patterns, the lines upon his face deepened as if reflecting the branching paths of destiny itself.

"The omens are unchanged, my son," Cathbad's voice carried the weight of mountains destined to crumble. "Deirdre's return portends a doom as dark as the raven's wing."

Conchobar's jaw clenched, the only betrayal of the storm within. A lesser man would have wilted under such forewarnings, but not the High-King of Ulaid. His resolve was iron; his desire, a forge that would not be quenched by the boiling waters of prophecy.

"Thank you, father," he replied, his tone as measured as the rise and fall of the tides. "Your counsel is the bedrock of this kingdom. But even the wisest may stumble in the mists of fate. You once foretold that Mesgegra, High-King of Lagin, would bring about my death. Yet it was not the Red Branch that shattered his armies, and Conall Cernach who laid his severed head at my feet? Perhaps the gods whisper, but it is we who decide how loudly to listen."

Without awaiting a response, Conchobar turned and strode back toward the great hall. The druid's words lingered behind him like wraiths in the mist, yet they could not sway the course he had chosen.

As the king re-entered the great round hall, a hush descended upon the gathered throngs. They parted before him, a sea yielding to the passage of a formidable ship. His presence commanded their attention as he ascended the dais once more, his gaze sweeping over the faces of nobles and warriors alike.

"Good people of Ulaid," Conchobar's voice boomed across the hall, each syllable ringing with the authority of his throne, "I have weighed your desires against the dire prophecies spoken of Deirdre and Naoise. And I have decided."

"Many years ago, mistakes were made and lives were lost. My sister, Queen Ailbhé and King Uisneach, were taking away needlessly," he said as he glared at Éogan.

A collective breath was drawn, held captive by the moment's gravity.

"By my right as the high-king, and with the blessings of Lugh and Macha, I hereby announce my intention to invite the exiles back to our lands!"

The reaction was immediate, a cacophony of gasps and murmurs rippling through the crowd like shockwaves from an earthquake. For a brief moment, Fedlimid dared to feel hope. Dáire, however, stood rigid, his hand tightening into a fist at his side. He had no love for his father, but he would not see his bloodline dragged into ruin. His red cloak stirred as he shifted his weight, glancing toward Conchobar. He would fight for Ulaid, as was his duty, but if Deirdre returned, he knew war would follow.

Druid's Promise

Eyes widened, whispers turned into clamorous debate, and the very foundations of Cróeb Ruad seemed to tremble with the implications of Conchobar's decree. For the king had spoken, and though the threads of fate might threaten to unravel, his word was now the loom upon which the future would be woven.

Amidst the tumult of voices and the clamour of disbelief, Queen Mugain rose from her seat, her regal bearing now a tempest of wrath. A shadow passed over her face, the kind that precedes a storm on the horizon. Her auburn hair, once a cascade of elegance, seemed to crackle with the fire of her indignation. The opulent folds of her gown whispered against the stone floor as she moved, her piercing green eyes fixed on Conchobar.

"Have you lost all sense?" Her voice cut through the din, sharp as the edge of a sword. "Your obsession with this girl has driven you to madness. I will not witness the ruin of everything we have built." She did not wait for an answer, nor did she spare another glance at the assembly. With a fluidity that belied the tension coiled within her frame, Mugain exited the hall, her departure leaving a wake of silent awe. Conchobar stood motionless, the queen's challenge hanging in the air like the scent of lightning-struck oak.

In the void left by the queen's exit, Éogan mac Durthacht found his opportunity. His broad shoulders shifted as he stepped forward, the light of the great hall glinting off his golden torc. His grin unfurled slowly, revealing the predator within, his cold eyes reflecting a purpose darkened by the shadows of past grudges.

"Allow me, my king," Éogan's voice was a low growl, "to bring back the exiles."

His words were met with a murmur of unease. Many remembered the old bitterness that festered between Éogan and Naoise; it was a wound never allowed to heal, a thirst for vengeance unslaked.

Conchobar's response came swift as a hawk's descent. "No," he said, his tone brooking no dispute. "This task requires a hand untainted by personal vendetta." He held Éogan's gaze, steeling himself against the other man's barely concealed fury.

Éogan's smile vanished, replaced by a hard line of displeasure. Yet he bowed, albeit stiffly, conceding to the will of the high-king. In this hall, under the watchful eyes of gods and men, even the desire for retribution must yield to royal command.

The crowd, still reeling from Mugain's dramatic departure, now processed the rejection of Éogan's offer. Whispers snaked through the throng, speculation breeding upon the lips of noble and commoner alike. Conchobar stood firm amid the eddies of uncertainty, his choice made beneath the heavy cloak of impending prophecy and the weight of his kingdom.

Druid's Promise

The great hall of Cróeb Ruad sagged under a silence that felt as though it had mass, as if the very air grew heavy with the weight of unspoken fears and unvoiced desires. In the wake of Queen Mugain's tempestuous exit and Éogan's rebuffed ambition, eyes turned, searching for a resolve strong enough to pierce the tension.

It was Conall mac Amargin who stepped forward next, his face had a rugged charm, sporting a moustache and long blonde hair that was shaved at the sides. The proud tilt of his head belied the turmoil within; his blue eye shone like the summer sky, while his burnt black eye seemed to absorb all light, reflecting the duality of his burdened soul. His voice, when he spoke, carried the weight of his past deeds, each word measured against the scales of honour and loyalty.

"King Conchobar," Conall began, "I offer my sword and my shield, to bring home those lost to us. Let me make amends for the evils of the past."

A collective breath seemed to be held within the walls of the hall, yet Conchobar remained unmoved. The king's gaze, unreadable as the depths of Loch nEathach, bore into Conall. "Your valour, Conall, has never been in question," he said, his voice echoing off the stone. "Yet the blood you've spilled still cries out from the soil of Clan Uisneach. Your hand, however noble, would stoke fires we cannot afford to burn."

Conall's mouth set in a hard line, his jaw tensing with the sting of refusal. He bowed his head, the gesture one of respect rather than submission, and retreated to his seat amidst the assembly.

The silence deepened, stretching on like the endless green hills beyond the fortress walls. It clung to the skin, crawled down the throats of those gathered, leaving a taste of discomfort in its wake. Not a soul stirred, not a warrior nor a noble dared to fill the void left by Conall's failed plea.

From the shadowed recesses of the hall, a tall figure emerged, a giant amongst men. Fergus mac Róich moved with a reluctant determination, his presence commanding attention as naturally as the Dagda commands the seasons. Scars etched across his weathered visage told tales of battles long past, and his blue eyes, once reminiscent of a cloudless day, now reflected the stormy seas churned up by Manannán's wrath.

"King Conchobar, I will go. I will bring home Deirdre and Naoise," Fergus's voice rumbled, steady as the roll of distant thunder. "But be warned, they are under my protection and no hurt will come to them. If even a single hair on their heads is harmed, I will shorten the life of the man responsible."

He stood there, a pillar of strength, yet his brow creased ever so slightly, revealing the gravity of his decision. He knew well the prophecy's dire warnings, the precarious balance upon which peace perched. But Fergus mac Róich was no stranger to navigating the treacherous currents of fate. If Ulaid's unity hung in the balance, then on his shoulders, broad as an oak, would rest the task of mending what had been torn asunder.

Conchobar's gaze lingered upon Fergus, as if seeing the former high-king for the first time since his bold declaration. The silence hung heavy over Cróeb Ruad, the feast of Lughnasadh now a distant echo amidst the gravity of the moment. Conchobar rose, straightening his broad shoulders, his fair hair flecked with grey catching the light of the flickering hearth fires.

"Your offer is accepted, Fergus mac Róich," he announced with a voice that commanded the hall, yet bore an undercurrent of respect few had ever heard. "Your valour and wisdom have long been the bedrock upon which Ulaid stands. I entrust this task to you, fully aware of your capabilities." The king's hand rested on the carving of the goddess as he made his vow, "I promise, under Macha's benevolent watch, that they will come to no harm."

A collective breath seemed to be released from the gathered assembly, a palpable sense of relief mingling with a taut apprehension. Murmurs filled the hall as eyes turned towards the towering figure of Fergus, who nodded solemnly in acceptance of the king's charge. It was not just a mission; it was redemption for the man who once ruled the kingdom four decades prior.

The crowd's reaction was akin to the rustling of leaves before a storm, whispers of hope fluttering against the undercurrent of unease. They wondered aloud amongst themselves, contemplating the return of Deirdre, whose beauty rivalled Áine herself, and Naoise, whose sword arm was blessed by Lugh. Their fates, intertwined with that of Éirinn, were soon to emerge from the mists of Alba.

Fergus scanned the faces of those before him. He saw warriors with grips tightened on their feasting knives, nobles with hands clasped in silent prayer to Morrígan for victory over impending doom. His gaze landed on Fedlimid mac Daill, his head bowed, weighed down by uncertainty, he would reunite father and daughter without conflict.

Then his eyes moved to Dáire. Unlike his father, Dáire did not look away. The warrior met Fergus's gaze with an unspoken challenge. If war was to come of this, he would not cower. The weight of Conchobar's promise was one thing, but the shadow of a druid's prophecy? That was another battle entirely.

As the great hall of Cróeb Ruad began to empty, the former High-King of Ulaid remained still, grounded like the ancient oaks that whispered secrets to the druids. Fergus knew the road ahead would be fraught with peril, but within him burned a fire that Áillen himself could not lull to sleep. With a heavy heart and steadfast resolve, Fergus prepared to embark on his journey to Alba, where destiny beckoned with both a promise and a threat.

Chapter 10

The Voyage of Fergus

The remnants of a hearty breakfast lay scattered across the rough-hewn table in the great hall of Cróeb Ruad. Fergus mac Róich pushed aside his plate, the meal sitting heavy in his stomach as he turned his focus to the weightier task at hand. His sons, Illann the Fair and Buinne the Red, were already on their feet, the urgency of their mission etched into the sharp lines of their faces as they gathered their belongings.

Illann's golden hair catching the light filtering through the high windows, while Buinne's mane seemed almost aflame with silent intensity. Their movements were deliberate, enclosing their personal effects within worn leather satchels with practiced hands. Nearby, their foster brothers moved with similar purpose, their youthful energy barely contained as they prepared for the journey to Alba. Sétanta's brown, chestnut and fair hair was tied back in a neat braid, while Lugaid's wild dark curls were pushed back by a leather headband. Both boys, though small, had lean, muscular builds, honed by years of training.

A shadow fell over the assembly as Leabharcham approached, her steps slow and uneven, as if each one carried the weight of years unspoken. Her silver-streaked hair, once vibrant, now hung limply around her face like wisps of morning mist. The warriors parted for her, their subtle bows tinged not only with respect but with quiet concern. Fergus straightened, troubled by how pale and shrunken she seemed, the once-indomitable presence now stooped with age and fatigue.

"May I have a word, Fergus?" she asked, her voice no more than a breath, rasped and fragile, meant only for his ears.

Fergus stepped forward quickly, placing a steadying hand beneath her elbow. "Of course. Are you well, Leabharcham? You look... worn. Ill."

She offered him a faint smile, though her eyes shimmered with something far beyond weariness. "I am old, my friend. The bones ache more than they used to, and the breath comes thinner with each season. I feel the veil thinning. Soon, I think, I shall take my place among the ancestors in Tír na nÓg. The call of that land grows louder in my dreams."

Fergus bowed his head slightly, the lines in his brow deepening. "You still walk among us with more wisdom than a dozen druids. The world will be dimmer without your counsel."

"In this world, perhaps," she said, her voice steadier now, though her hand still trembled in his. "But another waits. And before I go, I must speak plainly."

She led him into a side chamber beneath the woven tapestries depicting the legends of Lugh and of Balor. There, amidst the echoes of past glories, Leabharcham leaned close, her green eyes alight with foreboding.

"Be wary, old friend," she whispered, the faintest tremor betraying her concern. "There are whispers of deceit, dark murmurings that may threaten your quest and the exiles' safety. So much blood was split when Deirdre and Naoise escaped, I fear that there is more to come."

Fergus felt the familiar grip of apprehension tighten around his chest. He towered over Leabharcham, yet her words carried a weight that could bring even the mightiest warrior to his knees.

"Who is the source of these treacherous whispers?" he asked, his voice low and steady despite the growing unease.

"Gossip in the shadows of Éogan's court, Fergus. Shadows that move just beyond the light of truth," she confessed, her gaze unwavering. "Promise me you will guard them well, especially Deirdre..."

"By the strength of my arm and the edge of my blade, they shall come to no harm," Fergus vowed, the scars on his face hardening with resolve. "We march under the watchful eyes of Lugh by day and Macha by night. Their protection shall be our shield."

Leabharcham took his hand, her touch light but firm despite the tremor. "May their vigilance guide you, son of Róich. And may Dagda's wisdom grant you the foresight to see through the veils of deception."

With a final nod of understanding, Fergus returned to his sons, his heart heavy with the burden of Leabharcham's warning.

"Make sure your swords are well oiled," Fergus instructed, his deep voice resonating through the din of the Red Branch warriors coming and going. "It will guard your weapons against the sea air. We must leave nothing to chance."

His piercing blue eyes scanning the hall, as the clatter of preparations resumed around him. But Leabharcham's words lingered in the air, a silent spectre haunting the space between thoughts and actions, as the great hall continued to buzz with the readiness of warriors steeling themselves for what lay ahead.

He paused, letting his gaze linger on each of his sons in turn. "And more than blades, guard your minds. There are whispers of treachery, shadows that shift behind smiles and oaths. If betrayal comes, it will wear a friendly face."

The brothers stiffened slightly, eyes sharpening, but Fergus raised a steadying hand.

"I do not say this to stir your blood," he continued. "If it comes to battle, we fight, but you must keep your wits about you. A rash blade brings death faster than an honest enemy."

His eyes finally settled on Sétanta, who stood a little apart, fire glinting already in his youthful gaze.

"You especially, my son," Fergus said, his tone firm but not unkind. "Your strength is mighty, but rage clouds judgment. You are not a hound to be loosed, you are the storm held in check until the right moment. Do you understand?"

Sétanta's jaw tightened, but he nodded. "I do, Fergus."

"Then remember it," Fergus said. "In the heat of battle, hold fast to your purpose. Do not let anger drive your hand. We fight not for glory, but for those who trust us with their lives."

* * *

The morning air of Emain Macha hung heavy with a mist that clung to the thick thatch of the rooftops, suffusing the dawn with an ethereal glow. Fergus stood motionless at the threshold of the great hall, his broad silhouette casting a long shadow across the busy streets. With a final glance back at his father's hall where feasts and strategies had once flowed like the rivers of Ulaid, he turned towards the stables, his sons trailing behind him, silent as spectres.

Waiting for them was a young stable boy with fiery orange hair, some brightness in the otherwise dull morning.

"I've prepared your carriages, m'lord," he said as Fergus and his group approached.

"Thank you, son of Riangabar," Fergus responded graciously.

"Have you won any horse races lately, Láeg?" Sétanta asked of his friend the stableboy.

"Do I ever lose?" Láeg shot back with a grin, brushing some straw from his tunic.

Sétanta laughed. "When we return, we'll race again, and this time, you'll be left in the dust."

Láeg snorted. "You can try, little hound, but my horse runs swifter than your pride."

"Then it'll be a fair match," Sétanta said, clapping him on the shoulder. "Keep the horses well fed and brushed for me."

"May your journey be safe," Láeg said as he stepped aside to allow the party to enter. "And may you learn how to ride before you boast next time."

Two carriages awaited them, their dark wood and iron bindings stark against the pallor of the dawn. The horses stamped impatiently, their breath forming clouds that dissipated into the chill. As they loaded their scant belongings, the sense of foreboding that had settled over Fergus since Leabharcham's whisperings seemed to seep into the wood and leather, imbuing the journey with a portentous weight.

"Father, would not be quicker if we rode across country?" Illann asked, his gentle tone a counterpoint to the unease that writhed beneath the surface.

"Rushing leads to mistakes, son. And mistakes bear the bitter fruit of regret," Fergus replied, eyes examining the carriages as if seeking counsel from the goddess Macha herself, her protection woven within the very land of Ulaid.

At that moment the stable doors swung open, and Cormac mac Clothru, Fergus' former ward, stepped in from the gloom outside. Spotting Lugaid, he crossed the threshold with a grin and ruffled his half-brother's hair in passing.

"I've decided to join you all on this adventure. After all, it was my idea," he announced confidently.

Fergus studied him for a moment, remembering the trust he once had in his foster son. But that was many years ago, and Leabharcham's warning weighed heavily on his mind. Would Conchobar really put his eldest son at risk? Fergus thought to himself as he look at Cormac up and down.

"You can come," Fergus finally said after careful consideration. "I hope you're packed because we are just leaving."

The carriages creaked into motion, the slow turn of wheels punctuating the stillness of their departure. No fanfare nor cry marked their departure, only the soft murmur of hooves upon the earth and the occasional jangle of harness. They passed through the upper gates and then downhill through the lower walls, which encircled the hill of Emain Macha, before turning east, towards the sea.

As they traversed the verdant countryside, the landscape of Ulaid unfurled around them. Rolling hills rose and fell with the rhythm of slumbering giants, draped in cloaks of emerald and gold. Ancient forests stood sentinel, their canopies knitted into a tapestry of green that whispered secrets of ages past. Each bend in the highway revealed vistas untouched by time, as if the gods themselves had carved the earth for their own pleasure.

Yet, the beauty did little to ease the clenching grip on Fergus's heart. Each league travelled was a metaphor for his internal strife, the distance between what was known and the unknown perils that lay ahead. His mind replayed Leabharcham's warning, the whispered threats lurking in the shadows, and the responsibility he bore for the precious lives entrusted to his care.

"Are we being followed, Father?" Buinne's query pierced the shroud of Fergus's contemplations, his red hair a fiery banner against the green countryside.

"Watchfulness will serve us better than worry," Fergus counselled, his piercing blue eyes vigilant. "Keep your suspicions sharp but sheath them until the moment is ripe."

The sun began its descent, cloaking the sky in hues of amber and violet, as the procession made camp beneath the boughs of an ancient oak, its limbs stretched wide as if to embrace them. There, under the watchful eye of the moon, they found respite within the whispers of the leaves.

On the morrow, the carriages rolled onward, the second day's journey unfolding with quiet resolve. His home, Carrig Fergus, loomed in the distance, its promise of passage across the sea a beacon drawing them ever nearer. Fergus knew well the fortress that bore his name, its stones a testament to the strength and resolve required for the trials to come.

"By the grace of Macha, may our path be true and our purpose steadfast," Fergus murmured as the stone walls greeted them with the silent assurance of an old friend, steadfast amid the tides of fate.

The heavy oaken gates swung open with a groan that echoed the unease in Fergus mac Róich's heart. The fortress, steadfast upon the cliffside, had borne witness to countless departures, but few held such weight as this. His eyes scanned the courtyard, seeking assurance in the familiar, stones worn by wind and brine, the rhythmic clanking of smiths' hammers, and there, emerging from the shadow of the keep, his steward Dubthach Dóeltenga.

"Welcome home, Fergus!" Dubthach's voice boomed across the courtyard, his arms open wide in greeting. His wiry frame moved with a warrior's grace, the dark lock of hair falling across his scarred cheek as he approached. "Your messenger arrived during the night. The Red Oak awaits you, her sails hungry for the kiss of Manannán's breath."

Fergus's massive hand clasped Dubthach's forearm, the bond between them as solid as the earth beneath their feet. "Beetle Tongue, your words lift the spirit," Fergus said, his tone laced with gratitude and a note of solemnity. "But let us hope the god of the sea holds more than just wind in store for our journey."

A shared glance held the unspoken truths of their undertaking, the risks and silent prayers that cloaked their mission like the mists of Manannán himself. They turned together to survey the vessel moored at the quay, its timbers creaking in anticipation of the voyage to come.

"Walk with me," Fergus murmured, gesturing for privacy. Together, they strolled along the battlements, the sea's roar a backdrop to their counsel. "I fear treachery, Dubthach. Shadows within shadows have been cast upon our path, and

I trust not the loyalties of those who might see our quest thwarted."

Dubthach's gaze flickered toward the horizon, where the realm of man met the domain of gods. "Will I muster the levies?" he suggested, his voice betraying no hint of the humour he was known for.

"Your mind is ever a fortress," Fergus acknowledged. "Summon them after we sail. Let Conchobar's spies find nothing but ghosts in our wake," the weight of command resting easier on his shoulders for Dubthach's presence. "We shall be as phantoms upon the waters, our true course hidden until it is too late for any foe to intervene."

"Then it is settled." Dubthach clapped Fergus on the back, a gesture that sparked embers of camaraderie against the chill of duty. "Let us make ready. The tide waits for no man, and neither does destiny." Fergus allowed himself the comfort of his ally's resolve, knowing that the road ahead, though fraught with peril, was not one he walked alone.

"I have one last matter to attend to, before we sail," Fergus said as they descended from the ramparts.

* * *

Fergus' boots echoed hollowly against the stone floor of the armoury, a cavernous chamber where the air hung heavy with the scent of oil and metal. His father's banner hung from the ceiling, displaying a magnificent red oak, with five branches like an open hand, on a backdrop of pure white. Wall-mounted torches cast flickering shadows over rows of meticulously arranged weapons, but it was to the far end he strode, to a case that held more than mere iron.

The Caladbolg, its name whispered in reverence through generations, waited for him, ensconced in blood red velvet. The sword's presence filled the room, a silent sentinel of immense power. Its blade was forged from a fallen star in Goibniu's mythical fires. The steel was folded and layered with intricate, swirling patterns that shimmered with the full spectrum of the rainbow and seemed untouched by the passage of time. Ogham runes etched along its length spoke of battles won and kingdoms forged, and Fergus felt the weight of his ancestors' gaze upon him as he reached out and took the golden hilt in hand.

The memory of deception clung to him like a shroud; Conchobar mac Nessa's treachery still festered deep within his heart. The usurpation of his throne all those years ago was a wound that never fully healed. But with Caladbolg at his side, Fergus would not be fooled again. The sword was the tangible legacy of his line, a symbol of his rightful place and the justice he would uphold. His grip tightened, determination setting his jaw in a hard line. Betrayal would meet its match this day.

Holding it before him, he bowed his head. "Caladbolg," he said, voice low but firm, "I swear this to you, Deirdre and Naoise shall come to no harm under my watch. Their journey will end in peace, or I shall not see the end of mine."

He paused, the oath settling like iron in his chest. "I pray your edge stays sheathed, that no blood need fall. But if Conchobar's treachery stirs again in Emain Macha, if his lust rises to claim new lives, then let this blade be their shield. Not for vengeance, but for protection. Not for wrath, but for what is right."

He lowered the sword, its point grazing the earth. "For their safety, for the word I gave, and the honour that binds me still. I will stand. I will not break."

* * *

The sea's expanse stretched before them, grey and foreboding, as Fergus led his sons down to where their galley awaited, moored and rocking gently against the quay. The group were sombre, each lost in thoughts of the mission ahead, of alliances and enmity, of love sought and sanctuary promised.

They boarded in silence, the only sound the creak of wood and the slap of water against the hull. Sailors scurried about, securing cargo and preparing for departure, their movements swift and sure under Fergus' watchful eye.

Gelbann, the wiry captain of the Red Oak, approached Fergus and said, "What are your orders, m'lord?"

"We will sail north until we reach Dún Borrach, perched atop the rocky cliffs, then head northwest across the sea," Fergus instructed.

Gelbann nodded in acknowledgement, "And where do we go once we reach Alba's shores?"

"We'll then sail along the coast of Cionn Tíre until we reach our destination, Loch Eite, the haven of the exiles," Fergus answered.

"Understood," Gelbann said, with a strange glimmer in his eyes.

As the sail unfurled, the red embroidered oak tree was revealed as it caught the breath of the sea, the Red Oak began to ease away from Carrig Fergus, leaving behind the familiar for the uncertain whispers of fate.

"Keep her steady," Fergus commanded, his voice carrying the authority of one who had known the clash of shield and spear, the rally of men, and the quiet dread of strategy.

The oars dipped into the churning waters, rowers' muscles tensing and relaxing in practiced rhythm. Above them, the sky brooded, clouds massing on the horizon like an army in wait. Fergus could feel the tension in the air, the unspoken anticipation of the storm that lurked beyond sight but not beyond sense.

Chapter 11

Peace Disturbed

A raven's call echoed through Deirdre's troubled dreams, its mournful cry a harbinger of ill tidings. She startled awake, her heart pounding in the pre-dawn stillness. Beside her, Aífe sat up, eyes wide with fear.

"Mother, I dreamt of a raven from Ulaid," Aífe whispered, her voice trembling. "It came bearing honey, sweet promises dripping from its beak. But when it returned..." She swallowed hard. "Blood stained its feathers."

Deirdre clutched her daughter's hand, icy dread seeping into her bones. "I saw it too, my love. The same vision, as clear as the moon's reflection upon the loch."

They locked gazes, shared understanding passing between them. The gods had sent a warning, and they dared not ignore it. Deirdre threw back the furs, her bare feet meeting the cool earthen floor.

"Let us go outside and I will heat the porridge. Some food in our bellies will do us good." She helped Aífe dress quickly, fingers fumbling with the laces as urgency thrummed through her veins.

As they emerged from the roundhouse, the first light of dawn crept over the hills, painting the sky in shades of crimson and gold. But Deirdre's attention was torn from the sunrise by a sight that froze the blood in her veins.

A single galley glided across the placid surface of the loch, its sail unfurled and emblazoned with the unmistakable red oak of the Red Branch warriors. Aífe gripped Deirdre's hand tighter, a small gasp escaping her lips.

"They've come for us, haven't they?" Aífe's voice quavered, but her chin lifted in defiance. "Just like in our dreams."

Deirdre's mind raced, calculations and contingencies swirling like leaves caught in an autumn gale. She had long imagined this day would come, but she just put those fears behind her. Now they had finally found a measure of peace in their exile.

She turned to Aífe, grasping her shoulders firmly. "Listen to me carefully, my brave girl. We must wake your father and uncles with haste. Whatever happens, stay close and do exactly as we say. We will keep you safe, I swear it by the Morrígan herself."

Aífe nodded solemnly, the trust in her eyes unwavering despite the fear that lurked beneath. Together they hurried back to the roundhouse, Deirdre's heart a war drum pounding in her chest.

The raven's message echoed in her mind, an omen of blood and betrayal.

As she hurried inside to rouse Naoise, a single thought crystallized with painful clarity. Their idyllic life on the shores of Loch Eite had come to an end. The past had finally caught up with them, and now they must fight or flee once more. Deirdre steeled herself for the battle to come, determined to protect her family at any cost. She would not let the dark prophecy claim them without a fight.

* * *

Fergus's boots sank into the soft sand as he stepped from the galley, the shallow waters of the loch lapping at his calves. His hand rested on the hilt of his sword, an instinctive gesture born from years of warfare. Behind him, his sons and the young kerns Sétanta and Lugaid disembarked, their faces set with determination, with Cormac following last.

The roundhouses stood silent and seemingly deserted, a far cry from the lively home Fergus expected. He motioned for his party to spread out, their steps purposeful as they approached the largest structure. The only sound was the gentle creak of leather and the soft clink of metal as they moved.

Fergus paused at the entrance, his heart heavy with the weight of his duty. He had sworn an oath to Conchobar, to bring the exiles back to Ulaid. But he had also made a promise to protect them from harm. The conflicting loyalties tore at him, but he knew he must press forward.

With a deep breath, he ducked inside the roundhouse, his eyes adjusting to the dim interior. The hearth was warm, the ashes recently extinguished.

"They're gone," Sétanta said, his voice tinged with disappointment. "We've come too late."

Fergus shook his head, his gaze sweeping the roundhouse for any sign of the exiles. "No, they were here recently."

"They must have seen the galley on the loch and fled to the wilds," Cormac added.

He moved out of the roundhouse, his mind racing with possibilities. If Deirdre and Naoise had fled, they would seek sanctuary in the wilderness. But where? The mountains? The ancient forests? He needed to think like them, to anticipate their next move.

As he searched for clues, Fergus couldn't shake the sense of unease that clung to him like a shadow. The druid's prophecy of blood and betrayal hung heavy in the air, a dark omen of the trials to come. He knew he must find the exiles quickly, before Conchobar's patience ran out and the fragile peace shattered like a brittle blade.

But even as he hunted for his quarry, Fergus couldn't help but wonder if he was doing the right thing. Was he leading the exiles to safety or to their doom? The question haunted him, a spectre of doubt that refused to be banished. He could only hope that when the time came, he would have the strength to choose the path of honour, no matter the cost.

* * *

Concealed within the verdant embrace of the pine forest, Naoise crouched among the dense underbrush, his sea-grey eyes fixed upon their home. Beside him, Deirdre, Aífe, Ardan, and Ainnle waited with bated breath, their hearts pounding in unison as they watched the scene unfold.

As Fergus emerged from the roundhouse, his towering frame silhouetted against the pale morning light, Naoise felt a flicker of recognition. The weathered face, the grizzled beard streaked with grey, there was no mistaking the legendary warrior.

The two men followed Fergus, had his features, though one was red haired and the other fair, must be his sons Buinne and Illann, both great warriors in their own right.

And then, Naoise's gaze fell upon two unfamiliar figures, mere boys on the cusp of manhood. One, with hair of light brown, blood red, and golden yellow, moved with a lithe grace that belied his youth. The other, slighter and wiry, radiated a fierce determination as he scanned the surroundings with bright, curious eyes.

But it was the presence of Conchobar's son Cormac that sent a tremor of unease through Naoise's being.

"Deirdre! Naoise!" Fergus's voice rang out, shattering the stillness of the forest. The sound echoed through the trees, a resonant call that seemed to carry the weight of fate itself. Naoise felt Deirdre's hand tighten around his own, her slender fingers trembling with a mix of fear and anticipation.

Again, Fergus called their names, his tone laced with an urgency that sent a shiver down Naoise's spine. The exiles remained motionless, scarcely daring to breathe as they waited for the warrior's next move. A third time, Fergus's voice pierced the air, a final plea that hung suspended in the morning mist.

Naoise closed his eyes, his mind a tempest of conflicting thoughts and emotions. To reveal himself would be to risk everything, his life, his love, his family. But to remain hidden was to condemn them all to a fate of endless running, forever hunted by the spectres of their past.

In that moment, Naoise made his decision. Turning to family, he spoke in a low, urgent whisper. "If anything happens to me, you must flee to Dún Ad. King Árd-Greimne will grant you sanctuary."

Deirdre's eyes widened, a protest forming on her lips, but Naoise silenced her with a gentle touch. "I must do this, my love. For all of us."

With a final, lingering look at Deirdre and Aífe, Naoise rose to his feet, his heart a wild drum in his chest. He stepped forward, ready to face whatever destiny the gods had woven for him, a lone figure emerging from the shadows of the forest to confront the ghosts of his past.

He emerged from the dense foliage, his footsteps measured and cautious as he approached the towering figure of Fergus mac Róich. The weathered warrior stood before him, his piercing blue eyes widening in recognition, a mix of surprise and relief etched upon his battle-scarred visage.

"Naoise, my boy," Fergus exclaimed, his gruff voice softening with genuine warmth. "It has been far too long since these eyes have beheld your face."

Naoise inclined his head, acknowledging the greeting, yet his grey eyes remained guarded, a flicker of wariness tempering his joy at the reunion. "Fergus, old friend. Your presence here is unexpected. What brings you to my humble home?"

Fergus's gaze never wavered, his tone resolute as he replied, "I come bearing a message from Conchobar mac Nessa, High-King of Ulaid. A message of reconciliation and redemption."

Naoise's heart stuttered, a dizzying mix of hope and trepidation surging through his veins. Could it be true? After all these years, could the curse that had driven them from their homeland finally be lifted?

"Speak plainly, Fergus," Naoise urged, his voice barely above a whisper. "What is my uncle's message?"

Fergus's weathered face split into a grin, his eyes sparkling with barely contained excitement. "King Conchobar has granted you and your family pardon, Naoise. He regrets what happened, those many moons ago, he regrets the lives lost, the death of his sister and of course, the death of your father. He invites you to return to Éirinn, to reclaim your rightful place as a King of Cnoc Uisneach. Your exile is at an end, my friend."

Naoise staggered back, his mind reeling with the implications of Fergus's words. To return home, to rebuild his father's kingdom, to walk the hallowed halls of Emain Macha once more, to feel the embrace of his kin, it was a dream he had scarcely dared to entertain.

As his heart soared with the promise of redemption, a cold shadow of doubt crept into his thoughts. The memory of past betrayals, of whispered lies and broken oaths, hung heavy in the air between them.

"And what of Deirdre?" Naoise asked, his voice tight with trepidation. "What assurances can you give that she will be safe, that Conchobar's intentions are true?"

Fergus's expression softened, understanding etched in the lines of his face. "Conchobar has sworn an oath before the gods, Naoise, in front of the nobles of Ulaid. He will not lay a hand upon Deirdre, nor will he seek retribution for the past. His only desire is to see the Clan Uisneach restored to its rightful place."

Naoise closed his eyes, the weight of the decision bearing down upon him like a physical force. To trust in Conchobar's word, to risk everything on the chance of a new beginning, it was a gamble that could cost him everything he held dear.

And yet, the temptation was too great to resist. The chance to reclaim his honour, to provide a future for his family that did not involve endless running and hiding, it was a chance he had to take.

"Very well, Fergus," Naoise said at last, his voice steady with resolve. "I must gather my family. They deserve to have a say in this decision."

Fergus nodded, his eyes shining with approval. "By all means, Naoise. I will await your answer here."

"Make yourself at home, there is food and ale, enough for all," Naoise said as he turned back towards the forest, his heart racing with a tumult of emotions.

The path ahead was uncertain, fraught with danger and the spectre of betrayal. But for the first time in years, he allowed himself to hope, to believe in the possibility of a future free from the shadows of the past.

As Naoise reached the edge of the forest, his brothers, Ardan and Ainnle, ran over to meet him, their faces a mix of curiosity and apprehension.

"Brothers," Naoise began, his voice steady despite the swirling emotions within him. "Fergus brings word from Conchobar. He says his curse of retribution has been lifted, that we may return home to Éirinn without fear."

Ardan's eyes widened, a glimmer of hope sparking within their depths. "Truly? After all this time?"

Naoise patted his brothers on the back and said, "Let's go find the girls and head back home. We have much to discuss."

* * *

The warmth of the roundhouse enveloped Fergus as he stepped inside, the aroma of roasted venison and herbs mingling with the smoky scent of the central hearth. Naoise and his brothers, looked up from their seats, their faces a mix of curiosity and apprehension. Fergus took a seat by Clan Uisneach, his giant presence felt at Naoise's side.

Naoise's gaze shifted back to Ainnle, his brow furrowed in thought. "I know it seems too good to be true," Naoise continued, "but Fergus has given his word that Conchobar's offer is genuine. That he seeks to make amends for the wrongs of the past."

Ainnle leaned forward, his voice low and measured. "And what of Deirdre? What assurances do we have that she will be safe, that Conchobar will not seek to claim her as his own once more?"

Naoise felt the weight of his brother's question settle upon his shoulders, the same doubt that had plagued his own thoughts. He turned to Fergus, seeking the old warrior's counsel.

Fergus met Naoise's gaze, his voice firm with conviction. "Conchobar has sworn an oath before the gods that he will not lay a hand upon Deirdre, that she will be free to remain with you as your wife. He knows that to break such a vow would bring ruin upon himself and all of Ulaid."

Naoise nodded, the knot of tension in his chest easing slightly. "And what say you, Fergus? Do you believe in the sincerity of Conchobar's offer?"

Fergus placed a hand upon Naoise's shoulder, his grip strong and reassuring. "I have known Conchobar since he was a boy, Naoise. I have seen the best and worst of him. And in this, I believe his intentions are true. He seeks to right the wrongs of the past, to bring an end to the bloodshed and strife that have plagued our land for too long."

Naoise stared at the fire as he listened, desperately wanting to believe Fergus. He turned to his brothers, his voice ringing with determination. "I hope that we can return to Éirinn, to reclaim Cnoc Uisneach and our rightful place among our people. But if we go, we must do so with caution, and with the understanding that our trust must be earned, not freely given."

Naoise rose to his feet. "Excuse me, I must speak to Deirdre."

Ardan and Ainnle nodded, rising to clasp arms with their brother, their faces alight with tentative hope.

As the brothers began to speak of the preparations needed for their journey, Naoise slipped outside, seeking a moment of solitude to gather his thoughts. The cool night air brushed against his skin as he stepped into the darkness, the crackle of a small fire drawing his attention.

There, huddled around the flickering flames, sat Aífe, her laughter ringing out like a bell as she spoke with Sétanta and Lugaid. The boys, so young and full of life, seemed to bring out a side of his daughter that Naoise had feared lost forever, a carefree innocence that had been stripped away by the harsh realities of her attack and injuries.

He watched as Aífe leaned in close to Sétanta, her voice low and curious.

"Why does Lugaid sometimes call you Cú Chulainn?" she asked, tilting her head.

Sétanta chuckled, rubbing the back of his neck. "Well that's an old story. When I was younger, I was on my way to a feast at home of Culann the Smith, south of Emain Macha. He had a great hound guarding his lands. A fierce beast, driven mad by illness or the full moon. It attacked me at the gate, nearly biting my arm off." He rolled up his sleeve of his left arm showing the jagged scars left by the beast's teeth.

Aífe's eyes widened. "What did you do?"

"I killed it," Sétanta said simply.

Lugaid jumped in, grinning. "He didn't just kill it, he hit a ball straight down its throat!"

Sétanta shrugged modestly. "After that, I felt guilty. I promised to guard Culann's lands myself until a new hound was raised to take its place. People started calling me Cú Chulainn, while I was Culann's guard dog, and some people still do."

"Especially when he loses his temper and the hounds madness takes him," Lugaid added.

Aífe's mouth curled into a smile, clearly impressed.

Naoise felt a pang of bittersweet emotion as he watched the three young ones, so unburdened by the weight of the past. They represented the future, a chance for a new beginning, free from the cycle of vengeance and bloodshed that had consumed their elders for so long.

And in that moment, as the fire cast its warm glow upon their faces, Naoise could almost believe that such a future was possible. That the evils of the past could be forgiven, that the wounds of the heart could be healed. It was a fragile hope, but one he clung to with all his might, a guiding light in the darkness of an uncertain path.

Walking along the loch shore, Naoise found Deirdre sitting on the pebbled beach. The shadows danced across her face as her eyes met his. "Naoise, my love, the dreams that haunt me speak of treachery and deceit. The blood-soaked raven is an omen we cannot ignore," she said her voice trembling with urgency. "Aífe had the same dream, she too has been drawn into the druid's prophecy that has cursed my life."

Naoise's brow furrowed as he took her hand, his thumb gently caressing Deirdre's knuckles. "Deirdre, I understand your fears, but perhaps the dreams are not what they seem. Fergus is a man of honour, and Conchobar's offer could be genuine."

Deirdre shook her head vehemently, her golden tresses swaying with the motion. "No, Naoise. The gods have shown me the truth. The day the Fachan attacked, I had a vision, Aífe struck down on the shores of Éirinn. If we return to Ulaid, it will be our doom. Please, I beg of you, do not let the allure of home blind you to the danger that awaits."

Naoise's heart ached at the desperation in Deirdre's voice, her words striking a chord within him. His heart ached with the weight of their exile, the longing for the familiar fields and valleys of Cnoc Uisneach. But could he truly risk everything on the promise of a king who had once sought their deaths?

Fergus rambled along the shore towards them, his imposing figure casting a long shadow across the rocky beach in the moonlight. "Deirdre, I know you have your doubts, but I come bearing the king's word. Conchobar has lifted the bounty upon your heads and offers you safe passage home. Your positions will be restored, and you shall once again walk the meadows of Éirinn without fear."

But Deirdre's grip on Naoise's hands only tightened, her blue eyes blazing with conviction. "Fergus, I do not doubt your intentions, but I cannot trust the word of a king who once sought our blood. The gods have shown me the truth, and I will not ignore their warning."

Fergus hesitated, the wind catching the edge of his cloak as silence stretched between them. Then Deirdre leaned forward, her voice gentler, more fragile.

"Tell me, then... have you seen my father? And Leabharcham, how is she? Are my family well?"

A flicker of warmth passed across Fergus's weathered features. "Fedlimid thrives. He still holds court with stories at every feast in Emain Macha, his voice as rich as ever. The halls ring with laughter when he speaks. His name is spoken with fondness by young and old alike."

Deirdre smiled faintly, a wistful sorrow in her eyes. "That sounds like him..."

"And Dáire?" she asked suddenly, her voice quieter, tinged with longing. "My little brother. I haven't seen him since he was barely more than a child."

Fergus's eyes softened. "He has grown into a fine man. Strong, steady, and just. He wears the Red Branch cloak now and does so with honour. There is courage in him, and compassion too. You would be proud."

A fragile smile touched her lips, then vanished. "I always hoped he would be safe... that he would grow up unburdened by what happened."

Fergus's expression sobered. "Leabharcham, though..." He looked out across the loch for a long moment before continuing. "She has grown frail, Deirdre. Age has wrapped its fingers tightly around her. When I last spoke with her, she told me she feels her time draws near, that soon, she will go to join your ancestors in Tír na nÓg."

Deirdre's breath caught, her composure faltering for the first time. She turned from them both, her gaze fixed on the dark waves as though trying to see across them to Ulaid itself. "My dreams have warned me of danger if we return," she said softly. "But my heart... it aches to see her again. I cannot bear the thought of her fading from this world without one last embrace."

Naoise put his arm around her shoulder, silent, knowing there was nothing he could say that would ease the weight pressing down on her.

"She asked after you," Fergus said gently. "She still speaks your name with pride. You are in her thoughts, even as her strength wanes."

Deirdre closed her eyes, and raised her hand to clasp tightly around her crescent necklace. "The gods may send omens, but they do not understand the bonds of the heart."

Naoise found himself torn, caught between the allure of Conchobar's offer and the weight of Deirdre's fears. He trusted her instincts, knew the power of her prophetic dreams, but he also yearned for the chance to reclaim what had been lost.

"Fergus," Naoise began, his voice heavy with the burden of decision, "I cannot deny the temptation of your offer. But Deirdre's dreams have never led us astray. I must consider her words carefully before I can give you an answer."

Fergus nodded, his weathered face etched with understanding. "I respect your caution, Naoise. But know that Conchobar is not a patient man and his offer will not stand forever. You must decide soon, for the sake of your family and your future."

As Fergus took his leave, Naoise turned to Deirdre, his heart heavy with the weight of the choice before him. He knew that whatever path he chose, it would shape the course of their lives forever. And as he looked into the depths of Deirdre's eyes, he saw the same fear and uncertainty that gripped his own soul.

The night stretched on, the crackling of the fire and the distant laughter of the young ones a stark contrast to the tension that hung thick in the air. Naoise knew that sleep would be elusive, his mind consumed by the impossible choice that lay ahead.

But for now, he drew Deirdre close, his arms a shelter against the gathering storm. Together, they would weather whatever trials the gods saw fit to send their way, bound by a love that had defied fate itself. And in the quiet of the night, Naoise prayed to the gods for guidance, for the wisdom to choose the path that would lead them to a brighter dawn.

Chapter 12

The Weight of Oaths

Deirdre gazed out at the morning sunlight shimmering across the waters of Loch Eite, her golden hair dancing in the gentle breeze. In her heart, a fierce determination burned like the glowing embers of a newly-kindled fire. She turned to face Naoise, his bright grey eyes meeting hers with a depth of understanding only a true soulmate could possess.

"My love," Deirdre spoke, her voice soft yet resolute. "The visons that haunt mine and Aífe's dreams, they hold a portent I cannot ignore. We must seek Ethniu's wisdom before deciding our path back to Éirinn."

Naoise nodded, his strong hand reaching out to caress her porcelain cheek. "Of course, my love, your instincts have guided us true thus far. If a druid's wisdom can guide us, then to Dún Ad we shall go."

Fergus, ever the pragmatic warrior, stepped forward. "I agree, a druid's counsel is wise. But we must make haste. My galley stands ready to bear us swiftly across to Dún Ad."

"Nay, Fergus," Naoise interjected, his lyrical brogue tinged with a hint of pride. "Clan Uisneach shall travel in our own currach, until our trust in you is fully built. But your offer is appreciated."

As the group prepared for the journey, a palpable sense of urgency and anticipation hung in the salty air. Deirdre watched as Aífe helped load provisions into their sleek, hide-covered boat, the young girl's resilient spirit a beacon of hope amidst the uncertainty that lay ahead.

Naoise's brothers, Ardan and Ainnle, took their places at the oars, their powerful arms ready to propel them towards their destiny. Deirdre's heart swelled with love and gratitude for her chosen family, their unwavering loyalty a shield against the gathering storm clouds of fate.

As she stepped into the currach, Deirdre's mind raced with thoughts of the future. Would Ethniu's wisdom provide the clarity they so desperately sought? Could they find a way to navigate the treacherous currents of prophecy and emerge unscathed?

With a deep breath, Deirdre pushed aside her doubts and focused on the task at hand. Justice, bravery, and the unbreakable bonds of family would guide their path, no matter what challenges lay ahead. As the currach glided across the loch's glassy surface, Deirdre knew that together, they would face whatever the gods had in store, united in love and purpose.

The sun-dappled waves lapped against the skin of the currach as they cut through the sapphire waters, the rhythmic creaking of oars and the distant cries of gulls accompanying their journey. Deirdre sat at the prow of the currach, her golden hair whipping in the wind, her eyes fixed on the horizon where Dún Ad awaited.

Beside her, Naoise's strong presence offered silent support, his hand resting gently on the small of her back. "We will find the guidance we seek," he murmured, his voice a soothing balm to her troubled thoughts.

Deirdre nodded, drawing strength from his unwavering faith. As the ships drew closer to their destination, a flicker of movement caught her eye. There, in the harbour, a white galley bobbed gently on the waves, its snowy prow gleaming in the sunlight.

"Look," she breathed, pointing towards the majestic ship. "The Mute Swan, a symbol of both our past salvation and the hope that guides us forward."

Naoise's eyes widened in recognition, a smile tugging at the corners of his mouth. "A good omen, indeed. The gods are with us, my love."

As the ships glided into the harbour, Deirdre's heart raced with anticipation. She scanned the shore, her gaze falling upon Ethniu's small, thatched crannóg that nestled at the village edge.

No sooner had they disembarked than Deirdre found herself striding towards the crannóg, her feet carrying her forward as if drawn by an invisible force. Naoise and the others followed close behind, their presence a comforting reminder of the strength that comes from unity.

Ethniu emerged from her dwelling, her weathered face etched with wisdom and compassion. "Welcome, child," she said, her voice a soothing whisper on the breeze.

Deirdre bowed her head in reverence, the weight of the moment settling upon her shoulders. "Ethniu, I come seeking your guidance once more. Aífe and I have both shared the same dream, a portent of our path... I must understand its meaning."

The elderly druid nodded, her eyes shining with a knowing light. "Come, let us speak within. The answers you seek lie in the realm of the unseen."

As Deirdre stepped into the crannóg, the earthy scent of herbs and smoke enveloped her, a reminder of the ancient wisdom that dwelled within these walls. Ethniu settled herself upon a woven mat, gesturing for Deirdre to join her.

"Tell me of your dream, child," Ethniu said, her voice a gentle prompt.

Deirdre took a deep breath, the images of her nightmares flooding her mind. "We dreamt of a raven, its beak full of honey, a messenger from Conchobar perhaps. Yet when it returned it was covered in blood."

Ethniu closed her eyes, her brow furrowed in concentration. "The gods have sent you a warning, Deirdre. Conchobar's treachery runs deep, a poison that threatens to destroy all that you hold dear."

Deirdre's voice faltered for a moment, then softened. "Fergus told me that Leabharcham is fading. He said she is old and ill... that she feels her time is near. And ever since, I cannot shake this longing. I know what the dreams say, Ethniu. I know the danger. But I ache to see her again, to hold her hand once more before she slips beyond the veil."

Ethniu opened her eyes slowly, her gaze filled with a quiet, sorrowful understanding. "It is no small thing to yearn for the face of the one who first held you in her arms. The gods may give warnings, but they do not forbid love. Still, you must weigh the risk. The heart often sees clearly, but it does not always see safely."

Deirdre's heart clenched, fear and grief twisting within her. "I feel torn in two. The seer in me says to run, to keep away from Ulaid. But the granddaughter... the daughter... wants to go back, if only for a day. I promised her I'd never forget her."

Ethniu reached out, resting a hand on Deirdre's. "Then carry her memory with you, but carry it wisely. Let it guide you, not blind you. Grief does not cancel fate, child, but it may help you find meaning within it."

Deirdre nodded, her eyes glistening, her voice thick with emotion. "What must we do, Ethniu? How can we protect ourselves from the coming storm?"

The druid's eyes sharpened, her voice strengthening. "You must be strong, child. Beware the machinations of men, for they are often guided by greed and ambition. Trust in the love that binds you to your family, for it is a force that even the gods cannot ignore."

Deirdre sat a moment longer in silence, her resolve returning like tempered steel forged in sorrow.

Ethniu continued, "You cannot outrun your fate forever. You are bound to it, but Aífe is not. Remember your promise."

She would not let Conchobar's treachery destroy all that she had fought so hard to build. Whatever challenges lay ahead, she would face them head-on, armed with the love and loyalty of her family. "Thank you, Ethniu, for everything," she said as she embraced the old druid. "Farewell."

As she emerged from the crannóg, Naoise's concerned gaze met her own. "What did Ethniu say?" he asked, his voice tight with worry.

Deirdre squared her shoulders, her eyes flashing with determination. "She confirmed our fears. Conchobar's betrayal is imminent, but we will not let it defeat us. We must be brave, my love, and trust in the strength of our bond. And there is one last favour that we must ask of King Árd-Greimne."

Naoise drew her into his arms, his embrace a silent promise of protection and devotion. "Together, we will weather any storm. Our love will be our guiding light, no matter how dark the path ahead may seem."

As they stood there, the sun setting over the loch and the Mute Swan bobbing gracefully in the harbour, Deirdre knew that their journey was far from over. But with Naoise by her side, she had faith that they would emerge victorious, their love and loyalty a testament to the enduring power of the human spirit.

* * *

The great hall of Dún Ad hummed with a palpable tension as Deirdre and Naoise entered, hand in hand. Aífe, Ainnle, and Ardan trailed closely behind, their footsteps soft and deliberate on the stone floor. Bringing up the rear was Fiach, the steadfast captain of the Mute Swan, his presence a quiet strength requested by Deirdre herself.

The flickering torchlight cast elongated shadows across the stone walls, and the murmur of voices fell to a hush as all eyes turned towards them. At the far end of the hall, King Árd-Greimne sat at a long table, while Scáthach sat at his right hand, her horn armour glinting in the firelight.

"Come my friends, please be seated," Árd-Greimne said, his voice a rumble that filled the space between them.

As they took their seats at the table, the doors opened, and Fergus and his sons entered the hall.

"Fergus, my old friend," Árd-Greimne called out. "If I remember correctly, you are under geas that you cannot refuse an offer of hospitality. Come sit, it has been too long since we last shared a meal."

"You have a good memory," Fergus said with a smile as he approached the table, "Allow me to introduce my sons Illann and Buinne and foster sons Cormac, Sétanta and Lugaid."

Árd-Greimne responded warmly, "Welcome, sons of Fergus."

Fergus inclined his head, a gesture of respect and familiarity. The bonds of friendship run deep, he mused, even in the face of duty and loyalty.

As Fergus and his sons sat along the table, bondmaidens emerged from the shadows, bearing trays laden with food and mead. The aroma of roasted meats and fragrant herbs wafted through the air, a tempting distraction from the purpose that had brought them here.

Fergus leaned forward, his elbows resting on the table as he fixed the with a steady gaze. "King Árd-Greimne," he began, his voice measured and even, "I come bearing news from Ulaid. King Conchobar has granted Deirdre and Naoise permission to return, to reclaim their place among the people of Éirinn, and that the kingdom of Cnoc Uisneach shall be restored to Naoise, its rightful ruler.

Árd-Greimne's eyes narrowed, a flicker of something unreadable passing across his face. "They are my subjects now, Fergus. Their fate lies in my hands, not those of Conchobar mac Nessa."

Fergus nodded, his expression grave. "I understand, my friend. But I give you my word, my personal guarantee, that they will be under my protection. No harm will come to them, not while I draw breath."

Deirdre's heart raced, the weight of Ethniu's warning pressing upon her like a physical burden. She glanced at Naoise, saw the flicker of hope in his eyes, the longing for a peaceful resolution. But she knew, with a certainty that chilled her to the bone, that Conchobar's words were nothing more than a gilded trap.

"And what assurances do we have of Conchobar's sincerity?" Deirdre asked, her voice clear and steady despite the turmoil within. "What proof can he offer that this is not simply another ploy to lure us into his clutches?"

Fergus's brow furrowed, his eyes searching Deirdre's face. "Conchobar has given his word, and I have sworn to uphold it. My honour as a warrior is my bond, and I will not see it broken."

Naoise leaned forward, his hands resting upon the tabletop. "We have suffered too long under Conchobar's treachery to trust in words alone. If he truly seeks peace, let him prove it with actions, not hollow promises."

Deirdre felt a surge of pride at her beloved's words, but even though her resolve was unwavering, a flicker of doubt gnawed at the edges of her mind. Could they truly defy the prophecy that had haunted their steps for so long? Or were they merely delaying the inevitable, drawing out the agony of their fate? Is it time to face her destiny?

As if sensing her thoughts, Naoise turned to her, his eyes filled with a fierce love that took her breath away. "My love, together we are stronger than any prophecy, any king's decree. Our love will be our shield, our guiding light through the darkness ahead."

Deirdre nodded, her heart swelling with a love that transcended fear, transcended doubt. "Together," she whispered, her hand finding his, their fingers intertwining like the threads of their destiny.

Druid's Promise

And as they sat at the king's table, their love a beacon of hope amidst the gathering shadows, Deirdre knew that whatever trials lay ahead, they would face them as one, their bond unbreakable, their spirits indomitable.

Fergus stood up, his towering frame commanding the attention of all present. "Naoise mac Uisneach, Deirdre, Aífe, Ainnle and Ardan," he began, his voice resonating through the hall, "I, Fergus mac Róich, do solemnly swear an oath before the gods and all those gathered here today. I pledge to protect you with my life, to stand as your shield against any who would do you harm, as you journey back to Éirinn and reclaim your rightful place in the kingdom of Cnoc Uisneach."

He drew his great sword, Caladbolg, the blade a spectrum in the flickering light of the torches. "By the gods above and the earth below, by my honour as a warrior and my loyalty as a friend, I make this vow. May my father's sword shatter and my name be cursed if I fail in my duty."

The hall fell silent, the weight of Fergus's words hanging in the air. Naoise's eyes widened, the gravity of the oath stirring something deep within him. A longing for home, for the rolling hills and verdant forests of his father's lands, surged through his veins.

"Fergus," he said, his voice thick with emotion, "your oath honours us beyond measure. With you by our side, I believe we can face whatever awaits us in Éirinn. My heart yearns to see

Cnoc Uisneach once more, to walk the paths of my youth and restore the glory of my father's kingdom."

But even as hope blossomed in Naoise's heart, Deirdre's brow furrowed, a shadow of unease passing over her delicate features. She leaned forward, her voice clear and steady. "Fergus, while we are grateful for your oath, I cannot ignore the whispers of caution that plague my thoughts. I will not deny that I missed my father, my grandmother, and my brother. I believe now that the time has come for me to face my destiny head on. But I will not do so recklessly. The crew of your ship, the Red Oak, loyal though they may seem to you, are still men of Conchobar. I fear that their allegiance may waver in the face of their king's commands."

She turned to Captain Fiach, her blue eyes flashing with determination. "Captain, you and the Mute Swan have been our sanctuary in times of need. I ask that you grant us passage once more, that we may sail under your protection to Éirinn."

Fiach bowed his head, his weathered face etched with understanding. "My lady, the Mute Swan is yours. I will chart a course for Éirinn and see you safely to your destination, no matter the challenges we may face."

Deirdre nodded, relief and gratitude washing over her. She knew that the path ahead was uncertain, fraught with dangers both known and unseen. But with Naoise by her side, Fergus's oath as their shield, and the Mute Swan as their vessel, she could face the gathering storm with courage and faith, her love a beacon of light amidst the encroaching darkness.

Deirdre's heart ached as she gazed upon Aífe, her daughter's eyes brimming with tears. The decision weighed heavily upon her, a choice no mother should have to make. She reached for Aífe, her hands gently cupping the girl's face. "Aoibhgréine, my child, my treasure," Deirdre whispered, her voice trembling with emotion. "I must ask of you a great sacrifice, one that pains me more than any blade ever could."

Aífe's lower lip quivered, knowing immediately her mother's intentions, her small hands clutching at her mother's sleeves. "Mam, please don't leave me behind. I want to go with you, to be with our family."

Deirdre fought back her own tears, drawing strength from the love that burned fiercely within her. "I know, pulse of my heart. But your safety is paramount. The road ahead is fraught with danger, and I cannot bear the thought of any harm befalling you. I have foreseen that evil will befall you if you ever set foot in Éirinn, and I have made Ethniu a promise. Your life is fated to prophecy as was mine own." She glanced up at King Árd-Greimne, seated at the end of the table, his expression one of understanding and compassion.

"King Árd-Greimne, I ask that you take Aífe as your foster daughter, to raise her as your own. Here, in the safety of Dún Ad, to cherish and protect her."

King Árd-Greimne stood, his voice a soothing balm amidst the tempest of emotions. "Aífe Aoibhgréine, child of Deirdre and Naoise, I pledge to you my protection and my love. You will be as a daughter to me, cherished and nurtured as if you were born of my own blood. Your mother's sacrifice is a testament to her love for you, and I will honour that love with every breath in my body."

Aífe's sobs echoed through the hall, her small frame shaking with the force of her grief. "But I need you, Mam. I need Dad and my uncles. Please, don't leave me alone."

Deirdre gathered her daughter into her arms, rocking her gently as she had done when Aífe was but a babe. "You will never be alone, my love. We carry you in our hearts, always. And when the time is right, when the threads of fate have been woven anew, we will return for you. This I swear, by the gods and the love that binds us."

Deirdre's hand resting upon Aífe's head in a final, tender blessing. "Be brave, my treasure. Be strong. And know that our love for you knows no bounds, no distance, no end."

As she sat back down, her heart shattering with each movement, Deirdre watched as King Árd-Greimne gathered Aífe into his arms, the girl's sobs muffled against his broad chest. The weight of her decision pressed upon her, a burden she would carry for all her days. But in that moment, she knew that Aífe's safety was worth any pain, any sacrifice. The tears she had held at bay now flowed freely, a silent testament to the depths of a mother's love and the strength of a woman's resolve.

* * *

The preparations for departure were underway, a flurry of activity that filled the air with a palpable sense of anticipation and trepidation. Ardan and Ainnle moved through the bustling crowd, their steps slow and measured, as if each footfall was a farewell to the land they had called home for so long.

Ardan paused, his hand resting upon the rough-hewn timbers of the market hall. "It feels strange, does it not?" he mused, his voice soft and tinged with melancholy. "To leave this place, to return to a land we hardly remember."

Ainnle nodded, his gaze distant as he surveyed the scene before them. "Aye, it does. Alba has been our home, our sanctuary. To leave it behind... it is like leaving a piece of ourselves."

Their words hung heavy in the air, a shared sentiment that spoke to the bittersweet nature of their departure. For years, they had found solace and safety in the rugged beauty of Alba's shores and hills, in the warmth and camaraderie of its people. But now, the call of their homeland, the promise of reclaiming what was rightfully theirs, pulled them forward, even as their hearts yearned to stay.

In the bustling marketplace, Aífe stood with Sétanta, their youthful faces a study in contrasts, hers etched with the pain of her parent's farewell, his alight with the hopeful glow of budding affection.

"Don't be too upset," Sétanta said reassuringly, his voice barely above a whisper. "You will see them again. My uncle King Conchobar is a man of his word."

Aífe met his gaze, her eyes shimmering with tears. "Thank you, I hope you are right," she said, her hand reaching out to brush against his.

A smile tugged at the corners of his mouth, a gesture that spoke of secrets shared and futures imagined. "And you? Will I ever see you again Aífe?"

"I know we will meet again," Aífe said trying to smile back, "I can feel it."

"You will be in my thoughts, until we meet again," Sétanta said beaming.

Their words, tentative and tender, held the promise of something more, a connection that defied the boundaries of time and distance. In that moment, amidst the chaos of departure and the uncertainty of what lay ahead, they found solace in the knowledge that their paths were destined to cross again, that the seeds of love, once planted, would inevitably bloom.

Across the market, Naoise approached Scáthach, his bearing regal and determined. "I have a request, Scáthach," he began, his voice calm and measured. "A favour that I would ask of you, as a friend and as a warrior."

Scáthach met his gaze, her green eyes alight with curiosity. "Speak, Naoise. If it is within my power, I will grant it."

Naoise's gaze drifted to Aífe, his expression softening with the weight of paternal love. "I ask that you take Aífe under your tutelage, that you teach her the ways of the warrior. She will need strength and focus in the days to come, and there is no one here I trust more to guide her than you."

A smile touched Scáthach's lips, a gesture of understanding and acceptance. "It would be my honour, Naoise. Aífe will learn the ways of spear, sword and shield, the art of strategy and the power of resilience. She will become a warrior to be reckoned with, the daughter of Deirdre and Naoise in spirit and in strength."

Naoise clasped Scáthach's arm, a gesture of gratitude and respect. "You have my thanks, Scáthach. And my trust. I know that with you as her guide, Aífe will become all that she is meant to be."

As they parted, a silent understanding passed between them - a recognition of the bond they shared, of the trials they had faced and the battles yet to come. In entrusting Aífe to Scáthach's care, Naoise knew that he was securing his daughter's future, ensuring that she would have the tools and the tenacity to face whatever challenges lay ahead.

* * *

The sun had begun its descent towards the horizon as Deirdre and Naoise made their way to the end of the pier, Aífe walked between them, her head held high and her gaze fixed on the looming ship at the edge of the harbour.

As they reached the end of the pier, Deirdre stopped, her heart heavy with sorrow at the thought of leaving her daughter behind. She faced Aífe, her hands clasped tightly together in a gesture of farewell. "My brave daughter, we will return as soon as we know it is safe," she said, her voice thick with emotion. "You have been our light in this world of darkness."

Aífe stepped forward, wrapping her arms around Deirdre in a tight embrace. "And you have always been my strength, my mother," she whispered, tears glistening in her eyes. "I will miss you more than words can express."

Deirdre held onto Aífe for a few moments longer before releasing her and looked to Naoise. His eyes were filled with unshed tears, his jaw clenched in an effort to hold back his emotions.

Naoise turned towards Aífe and placed a hand on her shoulder. "My dearest daughter," he said, pride and sorrow warring within him.

"You are our legacy - our hope for a brighter future," he said taking the golden torc from his neck and placing it gently around Aífe's.

"This was your grandfather's, blessed by Lugh himself. Wear it at all times and it will keep you safe," he said as he kissed her forehead.

Aífe looked up at him with tear-filled eyes. She knew that this was not just any goodbye - it was a parting of ways, a farewell to a life she had known and loved.

And so, amidst the bittersweet farewells and the looming spectre of uncertainty, Aífe hugged her parents one last time before they embarked upon their journey, their hearts heavy with the weight of sacrifice and hope, their spirits buoyed by the unbreakable bonds of love and loyalty that would guide them through the darkest of days.

The Mute Swan floated gently in the harbour, her sails unfurled and ready to catch the wind, when Deirdre and Naoise finally boarded. On the opposite pier, the sailors of the Red Oak made their preparations for their return voyage to Carrig Fergus.

Deirdre stood at the white rail, her golden hair whipping about her face as she gazed back at the shore. Beside her, Naoise's strong hand rested on the small of her back, a reassurance of his presence and his love.

On the pier, Aífe stood tall and proud, her blue eyes glistening and golden torc shining in the fading sunlight. Scáthach's arm was draped around the young girl's shoulders, a gesture of comfort and protection. As the ship began to pull away, Aífe raised her hand in a final farewell, her voice carrying across the water. "May the gods watch over you, Mother, Father! May they guide you safely to Éirinn's shores!"

Deirdre's heart swelled with a bittersweet mix of love and sorrow. She knew that in leaving Aífe behind, she was ensuring her daughter's safety, but the pain of separation was a sharp ache in her chest. "Be brave, my darling girl," she called back, her words nearly lost in the wind. "Remember that you carry our love with you, always."

As the Mute Swan gained speed, the figures on the pier grew smaller, until they were mere specks in the distance. Naoise's brothers, Ardan and Ainnle, joined them at the rail, their faces etched with a mix of anticipation and apprehension. "And so we sail towards our fate," Ardan murmured, his eyes fixed on the horizon. "Towards the land of our birth and the trials that await us."

Naoise nodded, his gaze unwavering. "We sail towards our destiny," he said, his voice low and resolute. "Towards the fulfilment of the prophecy that has shaped our lives. But we do not sail alone.

We have each other, and the strength of our love to guide us through whatever storms may come."

Deirdre leaned into Naoise's embrace, drawing comfort from the solid warmth of his body. As the coast of Alba faded from view, she looked up to the moon in the night sky, "Watch over us Macha, as we journey towards the unknown. Grant us the courage to face our fears, and the wisdom to navigate the treacherous waters ahead."

And so, with hearts full of hope and trepidation, Deirdre and the sons of Uisneach sailed towards their destiny, their fates intertwined with the druid's prophecy and the machinations of kings.

Chapter 13

Crossing the Northern Sea

The Mute Swan cut through the placid sea, its snowy sails straining against the gentle wind as Captain Fiach guided the ship with seasoned hands towards the looming mountains of Ulaid on the horizon. On the deck, the crew worked with fluid precision born of countless voyages, powering the oars, coiling ropes and trimming the rigging to the captain's barked commands.

At the prow stood Illann, Sétanta and Lugaid, the salt spray misting their faces as they gazed out at the smudge of land on the horizon that marked the shores of Ulaid.

"It is good to see Éirinn's fair shores again," Lugaid said, unable to keep the eagerness from his voice. "

"Aye," Sétanta replied, a fierce grin splitting his face. "And we return as heroes! Bringing back Deirdre and Naoise in triumph. Ulaid will hail our names in glory."

"If they welcome us at all," came Illann's measured voice as he joined them at the rail.

Sétanta waved a dismissive hand. "You worry too much, Illann. We return with glad tidings and joyous news. Why would they not embrace us with open arms?"

"Because we also return with Deirdre, who King Conchobar still considers his promised bride," Illann pointed out. "Her elopement with Naoise remains a sore point. We would be wise to tread carefully, at least until we are certain of our reception."

"Carefully?" Sétanta scoffed, as the wind whipped his dark and fair hair about his shoulders. "The blood of heroes runs in our veins! They will heap flowers around our shoulders and bards will sing of this day from Emain Macha to Teamhair! You'll see."

But even as the words left his mouth, Sétanta felt a prickle of unease, like a feather brushing the back of his neck. Illann spoke wisely, as ever. There was no guarantee of the welcome that awaited them. He thought of Deirdre, standing pale and silent at the stern, and of the sons of Uisneach, whom the tales spoke of. For their sakes, he hoped his youthful confidence would be borne out.

A shout from amidships shattered the morning calm. "Stowaway! We've found a stowaway!"

Sétanta whirled, hand flying to the hilt of his sword. Beside him, Lugaid tensed, eyes wide. Illann was already moving, long strides carrying him towards the commotion.

At the centre of a knot of sailors stood a slight, wiry man with sharp features and dark, cunning eyes. He held up his hands in supplication, but his gaze darted about like a cornered fox.

"Peace, friends," the stowaway said, his voice smooth as honey. "I mean no harm."

"Then why skulk in the shadows?" demanded Fiach, meaty fists clenched. "Speak plainly, or taste my knuckles."

The stowaway flashed a placating smile. "My name is Gelbann. I am a friend of Fergus."

Naoise shouldered his way past Illann, Sétanta and Lugaid, his brothers at his heels. He looked down at Gelbann, eyes hardening.

Fergus mac Róich stepped forward, his towering frame casting a long shadow across the deck. His weathered face was inscrutable, but his blue eyes glinted with a mix of suspicion and concern as he appraised the stowaway. "What brings you aboard this ship Gelbann, uninvited and hiding like a rodent?" His voice was a low rumble, like distant thunder.

Gelbann met Fergus's gaze unflinchingly, a placating smile on his angular features. "I meant no disrespect, Lord Fergus. I only wished to ensure the safe return of the lady Deirdre and the sons of Uisneach. My loyalty to the high-king compels me to see this matter through to its end."

Fergus's brow furrowed, his doubts warring with the need to maintain order. "Does Conchobar know of your presence here?"

A flicker of something inscrutable passed over Gelbann's face, gone as swiftly as a shadow beneath the sun. "My actions are my own, m'lord. I assure you, I mean no harm to those under your protection.

Naoise stood beside Fergus, his blood rising. "You're one of Conchobar's spies!"

He reached for his sword, but Fergus caught his arm. "Naoise wait," Fergus hissed. "This man is under my service."

Naoise hesitated, torn between the desire to skewer this interloper on the spot and the tempering wisdom of his giant companion. He forced his hand to relax, letting it fall to his side.

"Speak then," he growled. "But choose your words with care. My patience wears thin."

Gelbann bowed his head, but Naoise didn't miss the calculating glint in his eyes. "As I said, I am here only to see you and your family safely home. The high-king wishes no harm to befall ye."

"And we're just to take you at your word?" Ardan's tone dripped scepticism.

"I swear it by the sun and moon," Gelbann said smoothly. "I am but a loyal servant, carrying out my duty."

Ainnle leaned close to Naoise, lowering his voice. "He could be telling the truth. If Conchobar truly means well..."

But the words felt hollow, even as he spoke them. Naoise knew in his bones that this Gelbann was a viper, not to be trusted. Every instinct screamed at him to toss the spy over the white railing and be done with it.

He met Ardan's gaze and saw his own doubts mirrored there. Ardan gave a barely perceptible shake of his head.

"We'll see soon enough if you're a man of your word," Naoise said at last, voice hard as flint. "But mark me, Gelbann. If any harm comes to Deirdre or my brothers on this ship, it's not Conchobar you'll need to fear. It's me."

Naoise turned away, signalling for Ardan and Ainnle to follow. They left Gelbann standing in front of Fergus, a self-satisfied smile playing about his thin lips.

Fergus studied Gelbann for a long moment, the silence broken only by the creaking of the ship's timbers and the whisper of the wind. At last, he nodded, his decision made. "You would be wise to heed Naoise's warning, Gelbann. But know that you are here under my sufferance. Any hint of treachery, and you will answer to my blade."

As Fergus turned away, his gaze fell upon Deirdre, standing at the stern. Her cloak's hood was drawn close so that only her blue eyes were visible, to shield her face from the curious stares of the crew. Strands of golden hair escaped the mantle, whipping about in the salt-tinged breeze. She seemed lost in thought, her gaze distant and troubled.

As the brothers returned to Deirdre's side, Ainnle voiced the question that beat against the inside of Naoise's skull. "Do you think he's telling the truth?"

"I think he's a snake," Naoise spat. "And I don't trust snakes."

Ardan sighed, rubbing a hand over his jaw. "Truth or lie, his presence here bodes ill. We must be on our guard."

Naoise nodded grimly. The sons of Uisneach had played their hand. Now, all that remained was to see how the dice would fall. He could only pray to Lugh and Macha that fortune favoured the bold.

* * *

Deirdre's mind raced, her thoughts as tumultuous as the sea beneath the ship's keel. The butterflies that fluttered in her stomach since they set sail from Alba only grew with each passing moment. She could not shake the feeling that some great doom awaited them, a fate written in the stars long before she drew her first breath.

Can I ever escape the druid's prophecy that has haunted my life? The thought whispered through her mind, insidious and relentless. What if by returning to Éirinn, I have sealed not only my own fate but that of those I love most?

She closed her eyes, seeking solace as Naoise embraced her, the strength of his arms around her. But even that comfort seemed fleeting, a gossamer thread too easily snapped by the shears of destiny.

Oh, Manannán, she prayed silently, if ever you have cloaked a mortal in your mist, let it be now. Hide us from the eyes of those who would do us harm, and guide us to safety.

But the answer was a harsh cry from above, a raven wheeling above the masts, its black wings stark against the gathering clouds. It circled the ship, once, twice, three times, its haunting call sending a chill down Deirdre's spine.

"The Badb," she whispered to Naoise, her voice trembling. "Morrígan is watching us."

The raven had once trailed Deirdre and Naoise in their escape from Emain Macha and in their travels across Éirinn. Yet they seemed to have slipped its gaze when they fled to Alba, but now, as they drew near to the shores of Ulaid, it seemed the goddess of war and fate herself had taken notice of her return.

Is this a warning? Deirdre wondered, her heart racing. A sign of the doom that awaits us?

She gripped the rail, her knuckles white as she watched the raven disappear into the distant mist. The unease that had plagued her since they set sail now blossomed into full-fledged dread, a sickness in the pit of her stomach.

Suddenly, the world around her seemed to shift and blur, the colours bleeding together like ink in water. Deirdre gasped, staggering back from the rail as a vision overtook her, more vivid and terrifying than any she had ever known.

She saw Cróeb Ruad, the great hall of the Red Branch, engulfed in flames. The timbers crackled and groaned as the fire consumed them, the heat searing her skin even from afar. Smoke filled her lungs, choking her, blinding her. She tried to run, but her legs would not obey, and she found herself trapped, the ceiling collapsing in a shower of sparks and embers.

"No!" she cried out, the word torn from her throat in a ragged scream. "Please, no!"

But the vision held her in its grasp, relentless and merciless. She could feel the flames licking at her flesh, the smoke searing her lungs.

The pain was excruciating, a white-hot agony that consumed her whole.

Dimly, as if from a great distance, she heard the sound of running footsteps, the cries of alarm from those around her. But she was lost in the grip of the vision, unable to break free, unable to do anything but endure the horror that played out before her eyes.

At last, the vision released her, and she crumpled to the deck like a puppet with its strings cut. Her breath came in ragged gasps, her heart pounding against her ribs. Tears streamed down her cheeks, mingling with the cold sweat that beaded her brow.

"Deirdre!" Naoise's voice cut through the haze of terror, his hands gentle on her shoulders as he helped her to her feet. "My love, what is it? What did you see?"

But Deirdre could only shake her head, the words trapped behind the lump in her throat. How could she tell him of the doom that awaited them, the fate that seemed to shadow their every step?

We should never have come back, she thought despairingly. I cannot escape the druid's prophecy.

But it was too late for such regrets now. The die was cast, the path before them set in stone. All they could do was face whatever lay ahead with courage and honour, and pray that the gods would be merciful.

As Naoise held her in his arms, Deirdre cast one last glance at the sky above, searching for any sign of the raven. But the bird was gone, vanished into the mists like a figment of her imagination.

Yet something in her had shifted, as if the gods had peeled back the veil of the future and shown her only a glimpse of the torment to come. The air felt heavier now, thick with the scent of smoke that wasn't there, with the memory of screams she had not yet heard.

Only the bitter taste of prophecy lingered on her tongue, sharp, metallic, unshakable. It clung to her like a curse, an echo of things not yet spoken, of blood yet to be spilled.

Behind them, Alba faded into the mist. Ahead, the shores of Ulaid drew ever nearer, dark with promise. And though the sea carried them forward, it was fate itself that bore them toward a reckoning long foretold.

She tightened her grip around Naoise's shoulders, not for comfort, but as a tether, to remind herself that he was still real, still hers, while he yet lived.

For in her heart, Deirdre knew that this was no homecoming. It was the beginning of the end.

Colin Dunne

Druid's Promise

BACKGROUND

Druid's Promise takes place in Gaelic Ireland, in the 45th year of Conchobar mac Nessa's reign, shortly before the birth of Christ. Ireland at this time had a population of less than one million people and was divided into approximately 150 petty kingdoms, called túatha (singular túath), of between 3,000 to 10,000 people.

Each túath elected its own king from amongst the noble classes, choosing the leader with the greatest ability, unlike other European kingdoms where sons inherited the throne. The heir to the throne was chosen by assembly while the king was still alive in order to avoid succession disputes, with the heir apparent taking the title of Tanist.

The elites of Gaelic society were the nemed or nobles, druids were advisors, healers and tended to spiritual matters and brehons were the judges. Filí were bards who put to memory the tales and genealogies of the kings and nobles. In times of war, túatha would raise a regiment of warriors from the smallfolk, known as trícha cét (thirty hundreds). There were some artisans, such as smiths and leatherworkers, and there was trade with the rest of Europe for luxury goods. Each túath had a brigiu (innkeeper). Most of society was made up of the feini, which were the farming class, with cattle being the main commodity. The lowest class were slaves, bondmaids and bondmen, usually captured in raids with opposing túatha or traded like cattle.

Each túath, depending on geographical position, owed fealty to one of the five cóiceda (singular cóiced) or high-kingdoms, of Ulaid (in the north), Connachta (in the west), Mide (in the centre), Lagin (in the south east) and Mumu (in the south west). The high-kingdoms settled disputes between túatha, were focal points for seasonal festivals and spiritual ceremonies and provided mutual defence. Occasionally a High-King could, though force of arms, claim to have lordship of all Ireland and took the title of High-King of Éirinn.

NAMES

I have used the Irish names of the characters and places in Druid's Promise, and I have tried to avoid the use of the modern English names where possible. In cases where there were multiple ways to spell a name I have generally gone with the most commonly accepted version. The modern pronunciation is used in the case of Irish names of characters and places. Some of the more difficult names are listed overleaf with their approximate pronunciation:

CHARACTERS

Name	*Pronunciation*
Aengus	Ain-gus
Aífe	Ee-fa
Ailbhé	Al-ve
Ailill	Al-ill
Áillen	Ay-lean
Áine	Ah-nah
Amargin	Amar-gin
Aoibhgréine	Eef-grey-na
Árd-Greimne	Ard Grey-me-ne
Buinne	Boo-nah
Cairbre	Car-bruh
Cathbad	Ca-vac
Clothru	Clo-rue
Coinchenn	Con-shin
Conall Cernach	Conal Cear-nock
Conchobar	Con-co-vir
Cormac	Cor-mac
Cú Chulainn	Cu Hulann
Curruid	Cur-rude
Daill	Doll

Druid's Promise

Dáire	Dara
Dian Cécht	Dee-ann Kekt
Donn	Don
Dubthach Dóeltenga	Dove-tok Dool-tenga
Durthacht	Durt-acht
Each-Uisce	Ak-is-ka
Eochaid Sálbuide	Oh-ka Sal-bwe-ah
Eochu Feidlech	Oh-hu Fed-lek
Éogan	Owen
Ethniu	Et-new
Fachan	Fack-an
Fachtna Fáthach	Fack-na Fa-hock
Fedelm	Fed-elm
Fedlimid	Fey-li-mid
Fiach	Fee-Ack
Fiachna	Fee-Ack-na
Findige	Fin-di-gah
Finnian	Fin-e-in
Follomain	Follow-vin
Furbaide	Fur-bade
Gelbann	Gel-ban
Glaisne	Glash-neh

Colin Dunne

Goibniu	Guv-new
Illann	Elan
Láeg	Loy-ag
Laidis	Lay-dis
Leabharcham	Lever-cam
Lendabair	Lend-avar
Lugaid	Loo-ee
Lugh	Loo
Mágach	Mag-ach
Maine	Mane
Manannán	Man-a-nah-an
Medb	Maeve
Mesgegra	Mess-geg-ra
Mugain	Moo-in
Mug Ruith	Mug Ru-ey
Naoise	Nee-sha
Riangabar	Ree-an-gavar
Róich	Roy
Scáthach	Skaa-hock
Sétanta	See-tan-ta
Smóil	Smole
Súaltam	Sool-tam

Druid's Promise

Uaithne	Oo-en-ne
Uathach	Uh-hock
Uisneach	Ish-nick

Colin Dunne

PLACES

Placename	Pronunciation	Modern name
Alba	Al-ba	Scotland
Atha Cliath	Awe-ha Clee-ha	Dublin, Co. Dublin
Carrig Fergus	Car-ig Fergus	Carrickfergus, Co. Antrim
Cionn Tíre	Kun Tire	Kintyre, Scotland
Cnoc Uisneach	Nock Ish-nick	Hill of Uisneach, Co. Westmeath
Connachta	Con-ach-ta	Connacht
Cróeb Derg	Crave Derg	Bright Red Branch
Cróeb Ruad	Crave Ru-ah	Dark Red Branch
Crúachan	Cru-ag-han	Rathcroghan, Co. Roscommon
Droim Meánach	Drum Man-awe	Drumanagh, Co. Dublin
Dún Ad	Dun Ad	Dunadd, Argyll and Bute, Scotland
Dún Borrach	Dun Bor-ack	Torr Head, Co. Antrim
Dún Scáith	Dun Skah	Dunscaith, Isle of Skye, Scotland
Dún Sobhairce	Dun Sov-ar-ick	Dunseverick, Co. Antrim
Eadaíl	E-doyle	Italy
Earraghail	Ear-a-gale	Argyll, Scotland

Druid's Promise

Éirinn	Erin	Ireland
Emain Macha	Eow-an Mac-ah	Navan fort, Co. Armagh
Fáinne Chulainn	Fawn-ya Hull-an	Ring of Gullion, Co. Armagh
Fernmag	Fern-mag	Farney, Co. Monaghan
Lagin	Lag-in	Leinster
Leitir Ruadh	Letter Ru-ah	Lettercaffroe, Co. Galway
Loch Éirne	Lock Ern	Lough Erne, Co. Fermanagh
Loch Eite	Lock Et-eh	Loch Etive, Argyll and Bute, Scotland
Loch nEathach	Lock Nay-ach	Lough Neagh, Ulster
Lochlann	Lock-lan	Scandinavia
Manann	Man-an	Isle of Man
Mide	Mid-eh	Meath
Ruirthech	Roar-tech	River Liffey
Sgitheanach	Ski-ah-nock	Isle of Skye
Sionainn	Shun-an	River Shannon
Slige Assail	Sli Ass-al	Western Highway
Slige Chualann	Sli Who-a-lan	Southern Highway

Slige Midluachra	Sli Mid-lu-ach-ra	Northern Highway
Teamhair	Tower	Tara, Co. Meath
Téite Brecc	Tay-te Brek	Speckled Hoard
Ulaid	Uh-lad	Ulster

Druid's Promise

Colin Dunne

THE FAMILY OF DEIRDRE AND NAOISE

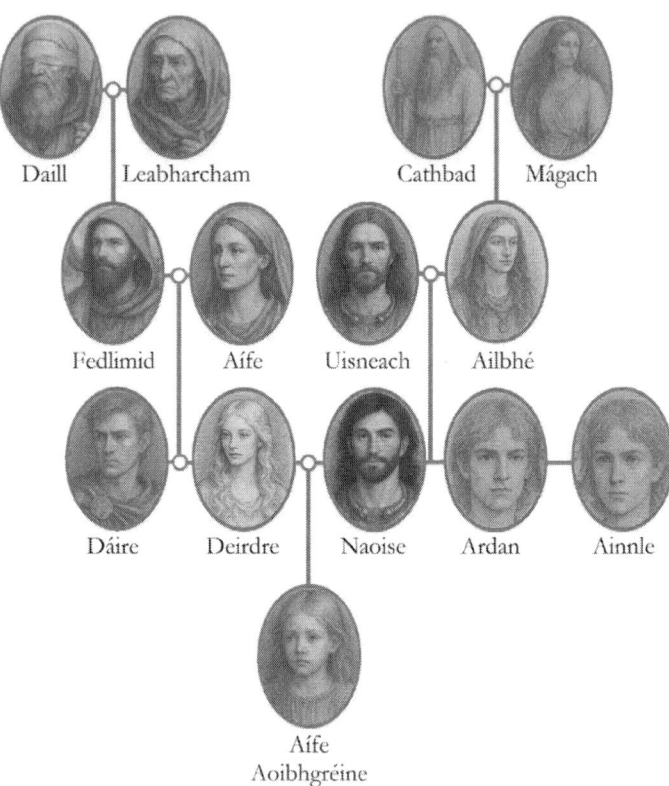

Druid's Promise

THE WIVES AND CHILDREN OF CONCHOBAR MAC NESSA

Colin Dunne

THE ROYAL FAMILY OF ULAID

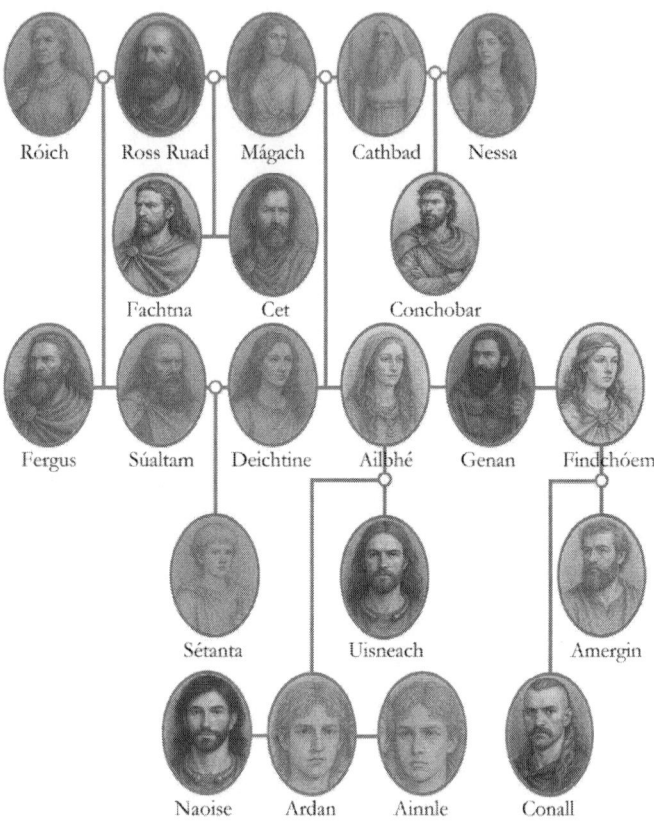

Druid's Promise

THE HIGH-KINGS OF ULAID

ROSS RUAD - Son Macha Mong Ruad, and grandson of Áed Ruad, Ross was the king of northern Ulaid. He alongside his brothers Cathbad the druid and Cairbre the Red Hand unified the kingdoms of northern and southern Ulaid, becoming its first High-King. Founder of the Red Branch warriors, he would lead his armies south to win the title of King-King of Éirinn.

EOCHAID SÁLBUIDE (YELLOW-HEEL) - Eochaid Yellow-Heel was the grandson of Áed Rúad, and father to Nessa. Following the death of Ross Ruad, Ross' son Fachtna Fáthach became the King-King of Éirinn, while Ross' cousin Eochaid became the High-King of Ulaid.

FERGUS MAC RÓICH - Son of Ross Ruad, and following the deaths of Eochaid Yellow-Heel and Fachtna Fáthach at the Battle of Leitir Ruadh, Fergus became the High-King of Ulaid. A man of great passion, he abdicated the throne in favour a seven year old Conchobar in order to marry Nessa.

CONCHOBAR MAC NESSA - Son of Cathbad and Nessa, and grandson of Eochaid, with a reign lasting 80 years Conchobar is perhaps the most well-known of the High-Kings of Ulaid and is a central figure in the stories of this time.

Colin Dunne

ABOUT THE AUTHOR

Colin Dunne was born in Dublin and developed an interest in mythology and fantasy at an early age.

His first novel Druid's Prophecy was released in 2024.

Druid's Promise is his second novel, which continues the adventures of Deirdre and Naoise.

Sétanta, The Boyhood Deeds of Cú Chulainn, is coming soon followed by Druid's Pyre, which will conclude Deirdre's and Naoise's story.

Email: colindunneauthor@gmail.com

Instagram: colindunneauthor

Printed in Dunstable, United Kingdom